ONE GIANT LEAP

Doctor Who

Meets

Quantum Leap

SIMON BURNELL

Please note this book is unauthorised and unofficial and no copyright infringement is intended.

Doctor Who © BBC
Quantum Leap © Universal
All pictures are respective of the copyright holder

One Giant Leap © Simon Burnell

ISBN: 978-1-326-27513-6

FUTURESCOPE

PUBLISHING

Now That's What I Called Music 1981

Sleeve Notes – Jamie Jones

Track Listing

1. John Lennon - Imagine
2. The Electric Light orchestra – Hold On Tight
3. Joe Scarbury – Theme from the Greatest American Hero (Believe it or not)
4. Grover Washington Jnr – Just The Two Of Us
5. Abba – One Of Us
6. Adam & The Ants – Stand And Deliver
7. Talking Heads – Once In A Lifetime
8. Queen & David Bowie – Under Pressure
9. Bucks Fizz – Making Your Mind Up
10. The Jacksons – Can You Feel It
11. Odyssey – Going Back To my Roots
12. Sheena Easton – For Your Eyes Only
13. Neil Diamond – Hello Again
14. The Who – You Better You Bet
15. The Police – Every Little Thing She does Is Magic
16. Journey – Don't Stop Believin'

17. Madness –The Return Of The Los Palmas Seven

18. REO Speedwagon – Keep On Loving You

19. Visage – Fade To Gray

Bonus Track
Orchestral Manoeuvres in the Dark - Souvenir

THE END IS ONLY THE BEGINNING

An Introduction by Jamie Jones

If you were a UK Doctor Who fan in 1989, then chances are, by the end of that particular year, you were pretty much devastated and angry all at the same time. Over the original 26 year run, the good Doctor had been fighting off various villains and monsters, but one enemy it could not defeat was the BBC itself when the axe was finally brought down on the programme. Fantasy and Science Fiction TV was pretty much classed as unusual in the landscape of British Television at that point in time and Doctor Who's life line had been diminishing ever since Michael Grade postponed the programme for 18 months back in 1985. This huge dark event had left Doctor Who with a stigma from which it never recovered, with ratings falling quite low throughout the run, with fans always breathing a sigh of relief when Who was recommissioned each year up until 89.

In America, however, the landscape was very different and science fiction had remained hot property with a slew of shows being commissioned to feed the frenzy of viewers all wanting a fix of escapist TV. One thing which America excelled at, was in creating unique formats and often some of the Sci Fi shows would mix quite heavy, serious dramatic themes with light comedy and adventure. Essentially the TV networks were trying to chase every kind of demographic they could in order to ensure high ratings. One such show was Quantum Leap which aired in the US in March 89. Literally a programme that had something for everyone from a heroic good looking lead in the form of Scott Bakula, comedy stooge in the form of acting legend Dean Stockwell and stories that varied from the adventurous and thrilling to the heart breaking and touching.

In 1989 whilst UK Doctor Who fans were deeply upset at loss of their favourite Time Lord, in the following year, in 1990, Quantum Leap arrived on UK shores. In a strange way, and when looked at more deeply, the formats of Doctor Who and Quantum Leap seem to have a lot in connection. At their very core, both programmes feature a time travelling hero who is a Doctor, travelling to different points in time, passing through, helping strangers and righting the wrongs and standing up for those who can't defend themselves. In both cases, Who and Quantum take what could be standard idea and make it utterly unique and unlike anything else on TV around them. Also Quantum Leap, like Doctor Who, also reached out to more than just your ordinary sci-fi fan because it was being watched by families who would sit down together to tune into the latest adventures of Dr. Sam Beckett. In a way Quantum Leap could easily be deemed as a contender for an American version of Doctor Who, if ever such a title existed. And maybe that is why, in 1990, a lot of UK Who fans instantly took to this new American sci-fi drama that was shown on BBC 2 from 9pm on the weekdays.

And now, in this very book you hold in your hands, is an exciting brand new adventure as the worlds of Doctor Who and Quantum Leap finally meet and cross over. Written by one of the very fans who grew up watching Doctor Who and Quantum Leap, this is much more than a story and more like a letter of devotion to two of the greatest ever time travel TV programmes that have ever existed. Sit back, as the TARDIS touches down in unfamiliar territory and Sam takes another leap in time...... Oh boy!

.1.
Imagine
John Lennon
1981

Imagine you are a spaceman.

Or indeed a spacewoman.

Hey why not? We are only imagining here, go wild, try something new. This is the enlightened 22nd Century after all.

2125 to be precise.

You are floating in the silent vacuum of space in this, near empty region, between the planets known colloquially in this galactic neighbourhood, as Earth and Mars. As you float there, with the roaring silence of screaming nothingness yawning around you, you observe...

Space rips apart. Contracts, and then spits out a small white, ovoid pod. The whirling chaotic lightning storm that is the Time Vortex can be briefly seen beyond the fresh tear in the fabric of space before it zips itself back up, leaving just empty black void and a dusting of stars. The pod speeds on through the nova speckled blackness. Serene in the silence, the man-made egg heads at speed toward its destination. Panning out now, the dusty paprika coloured sphere of Mars rotates into view. Like a galactic sized bowling ball rolling across the solar system.

But the Red Planet is not the Pod's destination you would notice. Rather, the trajectory would suggest, the jarringly irregular shaped lump of rock orbiting it instead.

Phobos.

The larger of the two Martian moons, arcs into the view of any observer that might be watching, and the small white pod can be seen approaching it at controlled speed. Of course, there are no real observers. That is the point. Secrecy is sacrosanct and the sole reason the Martian system was chosen at all was for its remoteness. Its solitude. Its loneliness.

Phobos. Named after the ancient Earth god of fear, orbiting the fourth planet of this system faster than its parent's own revolution. Unique conditions for the site of a unique project.

If you are still imagining yourself there as an observer, you might now zoom in on the pod. You would see that it is only a small craft. And a craft it most definitely is, as through a small, thick Nano-glass plated window, the pods single occupant can be seen. A man, probably in his late thirties, the speckles of heavy stubble on his face, half sits and half stands against a padded back support panel. From this side of the glass all looks calm and serene however, presently the man's face starts to contort and he appears to be screaming out in pain. Agony in fact judging by his expression. Should the observer possess such an ability, they could pass through the glass to the interior of the pod and listen to the man's screams...

'This means nothing to meeeee,........

This means nothing to me....... 'Aaaarrrrrrrrrrhhh VIENNA!'

The man, apparently not in pain after all, sings along to music coming from hidden audio speakers within the pod. After taking account of the small computer screen and the bank of input controls, there is scant room left in the pod for anything other than its single occupant. As the melody fades, another voice can be heard over the speakers,

'Very nice Colbak. I almost recognised a tune in there somewhere', chuckled a female voice over the airwaves. The man in the pod chuckled back and flicked a switch.

'Why do I never remember to switch off the intercom?' he laughed back. 'Did you like it?'

'The song or your singing?' came the earnest reply.

'The song! It's my favourite one from the acclimatisation media download for 1981. I'm just making the most of it in case it gets deleted from my head later. I think I was ok this time though, but the 1980's are a mad, mad place I can tell you. Oh but the music Sarsut….amazing! Anyway, you are a fine one to mock. It is well known at the Facility that you couldn't carry a tune in a bucket' The female voice feigned offence,

'Oi, watch it you! Just remember who it is that is controlling your descent here'

The man called Colbak arched his back as much as the pod confines allowed him and he raised his arms above is head in an ecstatic stretch. The journey back from 1981 wasn't a long one, relatively speaking, but the claustrophobic nature of these travel pods made it feel a lot longer. The female voice spoke again in warning, 'Anyway, don't tell me anymore, I've only just come out of one Sweep myself. I don't want another just yet. I am sending you the landing beacon now'. A low and slow rhythmic beep could be heard and it matched a glowing red pulse that appeared on Colbak's screen. Ah well, back to reality, back to work he sighed,

'Beacon has been received thank you Sarsut. Beginning my descent now'. He pressed a short sequence on a keypad by his right hand and closed his eyes as the automatic landing beacon guided the pod safely down into the facility launching docks.

This had only been his third mission, (so his records stated) and as far as he was aware it was a complete success. Obviously the Debriefing Scan would either agree or disagree with this, but he was hopeful that he would require little to no memory wiping this time. He hoped he would be able to keep the music though. The fact he had very little recollection from his first two missions suggested he had made some basic errors. His Facility Log records showed that he had been to 1999 and 1666 respectively, but all he could really remember from those was a computerised image of a bug from one and a strong smell of burning wood from the latter. Still, he reasoned, protocols were protocols and if he couldn't remember the missions, then there had to have been a good reason. He smiled again, flicked the same switch again from earlier and started singing once more,

'Don't you want me Baybeeee….Don't you want me Oh-Oh-Woaoh!'

If you, the observer, were still present, you could phase back out though the pod walls and watch from a distance as the small craft glided down to the surface of the barren rock moon. You would then see the pod passing over the large, distinctive *Stickney* Crater that gouged a huge eye-like impression out of the barren surface until a small collection of interlinked white buildings would roll into view, just beyond the *Kepler Dorsum Ridge*. The impressive crater, like an oculus, made the moon look, to some, like a kind of futuristic battle station. But then some people would think anything. The pod could then be seen to gently disappear into a small opening in the roof of one of these buildings. The large domed rotunda of the central complex building absorbed the pod, and a white hatch slid back over it, reclaiming the time ship back into the fold.

But there were of course, no observers. Not out here. Not in this reality anyway. Nobody to witness, for example, a small blue, box-shaped object spinning wildly through the Time Vortex. Destination unknown.

Instead, for now, we shall investigate further, what became of the small egg shaped Time Pod...

***

The smoke and steam cleared as the Tech Team scurried about like ants, attaching coolant tubes and data cables to the newly arrived Time Pod. Colbak watched them impatiently from within the Pod. He desperately fought the claustrophobia induced urge to burst out of his temporal eggshell. After five minutes of frenetic activity, the green light inside the pod illuminated and the welcome hiss of the pressurised seal release gave him his cue to push the door gently open and step out into the Launch Bay.

At last, a proper stretch could be had and he made the most of it. Relishing the ecstasy of his vertebrae gently easing apart as he bent down to touch his toes before reaching towards the Launch Bay ceiling way up above him. His exertions went largely ignored by the Tech Team. A crew of around a dozen engineers and physicists that were clearly and unashamedly more interested in the data he had just bought back than in the Colbak himself. They were right when they told him, at the Academy back on Earth, that there was no glory for the Temporanaut, only for the Project itself.

But there was something for the Temporanaut. Money. Landing this job at the Facility meant that Colbak was set up financially for a lifetime. Well , for several lifetimes actually. Widely regarded as the most well paid job on the planet, he was more than happy to suffer the occasional partial memory wipe and the apathy of the real thinkers in the building towards him and his fellow time travellers.

He walked over to the Bay's exit doors and placed his palm face down on the square pad reader. A quick line scan of his hand and the white door slid open for him with a whoosh. At the same time a fellow Temporanaut was waiting to come through, ready for his own upcoming mission. It was Pattro. He came to the Facility in the same induction wave as Colbak and the two men shook each to other's hands warmly.

'How goes it Pattro?' Colbak said with a smile, 'Where are they sending you this time?'

The other man was shorter than Colbak by almost a foot. His jet black hair was a mop of unruly strands which he swept back with a white gloved hand.

'Ahoy Colbak! My friend. Welcome back. I trust all went to plan. Well you are stood here now, so I guess it must have eh? Ha ha', he leaned in and whispered, 'I can't give too much away but they are sending me to 1492! Hush hush dear boy', he winked. Colbak laughed and waved his friend off as he walked off into one of the ante-rooms that splayed off from the main landing dome. The Launch Bays, each of which contained two freshly prepared Time Pods. He laughed to himself. Hush hush indeed? Any classified info would be wiped from Colbak's mind anyway in a moment.

He walked down the small corridor and into the Debriefing Suite. A sparse white panelled room that matched most of the Facility's décor, it was devoid of furniture apart from a solitary high-backed chair in its centre. Colbak walked to it and sat himself down. The lights dimmed slightly as the wall in front of him slowly displayed the image of the body-less face of the Projects' Artificial Intelligence Co-Ordinator.

'Welcome Back Temporanaut 425 Designation: Colbak. Please prepare for Mission Debrief.'

Colbak relaxed and closed his eyes. A beam of red light picked out a pinpoint on his forehead as the computer scanned his brain. Colbak felt nothing aside from a small warm sensation at the back of his head. Occasionally there was a small tickle inside his head . This he knew was a memory being erased. Some small element of the mission that the A.I computer deemed too risky for him to have knowledge of. This was all part of what he signed up for. The process was a short one and after about a minute, the lights in the room returned to full brightness and Colback opened his eyes.

'Thank you Temporanaut 425, Debrief complete. Total Sweep 0.25%'

'Yes! 'Colbak punched the air in celebration. That was by far his lowest score yet. He had been allowed to keep a lot of the mission memories this time, including, most importantly, the music! He got up from the chair and straightened his white uniform. He mock saluted the AI face as it faded back into the wall and walked out through the new door that had opened on the far side of the room, and out into the new corridor. He started singing to himself as he walked, *'Hoorah, Hoorah, Hoorah, Yea, Over the hill with the swords of a thousand men..'*

The corridor in front of him led him to a familiar intersection. Left or right. There was no choice of course. He was required to go right. Right led to the staff quarters and recreational areas. A shower, some food and more welcome, a bed. Left led to...well Colbak didn't know where left led to. A dull fuzz in his mind told him that there was a very good chance that he had probably asked the question at his Induction, and the thought had been wiped from his mind. Probably classified he thought and promptly stifled any blossoming curiosity about turning left.

Colbak lifted his right foot off the floor, making to turn towards his quarters, but froze instead. His foot hovering in the hair incongruously. Again, like in deep space earlier, there was nobody around to see, but if there were, they would see a pale, neon bright light flood over his face and down his arms and body. He went rigid as the electric light swept over him like a liquid before it dispersed, leaving no trace of it ever being there at all. Colbak placed his foot back on the floor and straightened his back. He tilted he head slightly to the left as if he were listening to a silent voice in his ear. With a small nod, he made a smart turn to the left and headed off down the white walled corridor instead.

Coming to a similarly closed door as before and with a familiar palm reader, he placed his right hand on the pad and passed through the now open door. The room he now found himself in was filled with banks and banks of computer processors. Wall to wall cabinets of quietly clicking hard drives and ticking routers that blinked at him with primary coloured diodes as he walked past them. The room was vast and cold. Colbak's breath plumed out of his mouth in wispy funnels of moisture as he stopped at an intersection of computer banks, listened for a moment and then made a right angled turn to his left. He paused again. Ahead of him, with his back to Colbak was a man. Dressed in an identical white travel suit , but distinguished as a technician rather than a Temporanaut by red piping on the shoulders. It was too late to remain un noticed though as the man turned at the footfalls behind him. Colbak walked up to the man.

'Colbak? What are you doing in here? You know the Processing Vault is off limits to... well, non Tech personnel' he sneered condescendingly. Like a viper, Colbak grasped the man's head in both hands and with a quick snap, swiftly broke his neck. As the lifeless body slumped to the floor, Colbak resumed his journey through the computer banks.

' Sorry, I'm not...myself at the moment' he quipped without looking back. He then added to the empty space beside him, 'Yes yes. I'll come back and deal with the body later. Calm down.'

After a few moments of seemingly random, yet deliberate navigation, Colbak found himself in front of a tall thin bank of processors. In stark contrast to the other whirring white units in the large room, this one was completely black. The Master Temporal Node Control Bank. He flicked a catch on the outside of the server bank cabinet and it swung open with a small squeak. Again he stood there, staring at the complex jumble of wires and diodes that were revealed inside, nodding every now and then at silent instructions. After about a minute, he knelt down and began removing cables with deft speed. Removing ends from one port and inserting them in others. Pausing every now and again to listen and occasionally muttering questioning words as if talking to an invisible companion, before resuming his cable rearrangement.

After five minutes of frantic work, Colbak straightened up and reached around to the back of the black cabinet. He stopped. Turned to his left and said,

'Are you certain?' He stopped to listen for the unheard reply, nodded and then yanked hard on the red cable that he had clenched in his grip. There was a momentary flicker to the flashing lights on the server in front of him, before they resumed their blinking. Seemingly satisfied, Colbak began to close the cabinet again. A small numerical display on the front now showed a countdown of numbers in small red neon. They blinked away as the black cabinet door closed over them.

72:59:37…72:59:36…72:59:35…

Walking back out of the room, Colbak's face smiled as the white door slid closed behind him. He slowly strolled up the corridor towards his quarters. Suddenly he laughed and turned to his left, addressing the empty space, nodding in agreement to an invisible companion and sharing a silent joke. He nodded a non-committal greeting to another Temporanaut as they passed in the corridor. He checked briefly that they had gone beyond earshot before addressing the air,

'Indeed. Indeed it will be. Now all we have to do is wait. I do hope it isn't too long before our Guest arrives. This body has a terrible ache in the lower spine. I shall be overjoyed to give it back.'

***

Three days later...

'But you are not listening!' Sylmac thumped the large round table in frustration. 'Look at the read out!' He sighed in frustration and noisily pushed back his chair as he stood up. He ran an exasperated hand through his thinning hair and walked away from the table. There were five others sat around the table, three men and two women. The man clutching the aforementioned readouts pushed them across the table for the others to see. He was a thin man with short black hair that was silvering slightly at the temples. His name was Davten.

'I can't be 100% certain. None of us can. That's precisely the point. But the medical reports are showing a progressive loss of base cognitive function. Each memory sweep is eroding our brain's basic....' A woman, sat across from Davten stood up, stopping his flow. She was an athletically built woman in her thirties with long brown hair worn in a complicated plat down her back. She spoke

'We all knew the risks when we signed up for this job Davten. The money is more than enough compensation for a little short term forgetfulness'. Davten looked up at her.

'Not all of us are here for the money Janfiel. Some of us signed up for the science. That notwithstanding, it's getting to be more than a little short term memory loss. There is a strong suggestion here that cognitive function and the emotional stability areas of our brains are also starting to be affected'. Sylmac returned to the table and leaned his broad shouldered frame onto it with clenched knuckles,

'That's not the worst of it', he said, 'Tell them about the build-up'. The other female at the table looked up sharply from looking at the read outs Davten had just displayed. She was Sarsut, and had just only just joined them in the communal area. Fresh from her Sweep after coming off the previous shift rotation in Landing Control.

'Build up?' she questioned. Davten sighed and lowered his voice to a whisper,

'I have reason to believe that there is a problem with the Time Processors. It seems to suggest a large amount of bio electrical build up. If I am right, then there is a chance of critical feedback and...' He was interrupted, this time by the man called Colbak, who was sat rocked back on two legs of his chair. Hands behind his head.

'If? If? Come on Davten, you can't be sure of any of this. We don't get access to any of the technical side of operations here. That Tic-Toc clown makes sure we are not able to tamper with any of the core banks...even saying that makes my head hurt. Restricted memory right there!' he tapped a forefinger against his temple.

'I have...ways to find out information Colbak. Keep your voice down. The last thing we need is more memory Sweeps than necessary'

'You have no actual proof we are suffering from mental abnormalities. Personally? I feel right as rain' Colbak retorted, stretching his arms behind his head and almost tilting back beyond the point of no return on his chair legs. Sylmac rounded on him angrily,

'Oh yeah. That's why I can hear you talking away to yourself in your habitation pod for the last few nights is it? Normal behaviour?' Colbak looked momentarily worried, before smiling back at the man across from the table. '

'I would thank you to mind your own business Sylmac. What I do in my own quarters is no concern of yours.' Colbak's eyes narrowed. ' Just what did you hear anyway?'

'Nothing specific. Just your voice. The ramblings of a lunatic. Are you saying that's your normal behaviour then? Doesn't surprise me'

'Gentlemen, Gentlemen please!' This was the remaining man at the table. Normally a very quiet person, Marstrik's utterance caused the rest of the room to look at the small ginger haired man. 'Davten are you sure about what you are saying? Are we really in danger here? I mean more so than usual' Davten sighed,

'I think so. Yes.'

Colbak snorted 'He thinks so? Heavens sake man! You have been working too hard. You are tired. Take a rest. Get someone else to take the next mission.'

'Colbak, the data I have is showing a large build-up of temporal energy in the Bio Filters. I fear there will be a huge feedback event soon if we...'

'We? We can't do anything. The Technicians run this place. Us mere Temporanauts are only fit for the dangerous stuff. The heroic stuff. We are nothing more than fabulously well paid cannon fodder. You are worrying about nothing. Fatigue is all...or maybe old age hmm?'

'Listen, if the system feeds back then the facility will shut down. No Time Pods will leave or arrive and the facility will go into lock down. You know the Protocols as well as all of us do. If it goes into lockdown then the McGregor Protocol will kick in and it will initiate the Final Sweep, facility wide. I don't need to tell you that it will be a 100% Sweep do I? '

Colbak stabbed a finger at Davten 'You are an old fool. The Project won't let that happen. Old. And. Foolish.'

'Sylmac is right, you are not acting like yourself lately Colbak. I thought we were friends'

'I am absolutely fine. Maybe I have just heard enough of your nonsense. I am not here to make friends. Only money. Come on let's go and get some food supplements. Leave Davten to get some rest eh?' The others apart from Davten and Sylmac followed Colbak out of the room muttering their agreement. Sylmac put a comforting hand on his friend's shoulder,

'Ignore him. Sod the lot of them. He's had his brain rinsed too many times. Besides, as my dad used to say, arguing with idiots is like playing chess with a seagull. No matter how good you are, the seagull is just going to crap all over the board and strut about like it has won anyway.' Davten laughed. Sylmac turned serious. 'When do you think it will happen?' he asked quietly.

'Any when in the next hour if I'm right'

'Then we are all screwed then my friend' Sylmac sighed.

'Hopefully not *all* of us'

***

In the silent computer room, the countdown that was instigated three days previously was nearing its inevitable conclusion

00:27:07...00:27:06...00:27:05...

.2.
Hold On Tight
The Electric Light Orchestra
1981

The Doctor whirled and waltzed around the TARDIS central console like a mad toreador dancing with a static electric bull. Flicking a button here and pulling a lever there and every operation delivered with an accompanying flourish of his unfeasibly long arms.

His companion, Amy Pond regarded him silently a few steps back from the console with a small smile of amusement on her face. Such a drama queen, she thought as he winked at her while pirouetting past on her side of the console. He twisted a dial, as if he were spinning a wicket-taking cricket ball delivery before spinning back, beyond to the other side, out of view.

'Why do you get so excited?' she asked him.

'What do you mean Pond?' the Doctor replied, his head bobbing out from behind the time rotor.

'I mean all this.' She waved her arm art him and gave a mock pirouette. 'All the dancing and the waving about. I mean it's not as if you are doing anything exciting. Surely for you, this must be like driving a bus?' she teased.

The Doctor stopped what he was doing and frowned at her in honest consternation.

'Driving a bus? Now look here Pond. I am piloting here, a multi-dimensional TT Mark 1 temporal transportation device through the truncated maelstrom of the Time Vortex. Aiming, I might add, to re-materialise at a fixed point in four dimensional space. On my own and', he added, and with a small cough, 'wearing a bow-tie. It is categorically NOT' he pointed a finger at her, 'in any way, shape or form…, like "driving a bus!"' He glared at her from behind a flop of hair fringe. 'And anyway, I am very, VERY good at driving it, so why shouldn't I show off a bit?' he ended sulkily.

Amy laughed. The Doctor may know how to operate a TARDIS but she knew how to push *his* buttons.

'Ok *Maverick,* so where are we heading then? I take it it's not to Oxford Street like we asked.'

'Like *you* asked you mean?' said Rory Williams, the erstwhile Mr Pond, coming down the stairs behind her, rubbing his hair dry with a red and orange striped towel. Amy turned and glared at him. Rory caught her fierce stare and froze like a gazelle caught in a lioness's sights. Rory paled, 'Right, yes. Like WE asked...I err...think I left the bath plug in.' He quickly disappeared back up the stairs and back into the bewildering collection of inner rooms of the time machine. The Doctor grinned as Amy turned back after watching Rory's brave retreat.

'I am not taking you shopping Pond. I can take you anywhere in the multiverse. Any *when* in the Universe for that matter. I'm not dropping you off to go around Harvey Nicholls while I wait here kicking my heels'. He fixed her with a look. 'The TARDIS is not the Number 22 to Putney Common you know ', he added and winked at her. 'I am taking you to 2125.'

'Humph! What's in 2125?' Amy asked, folding her arms petulantly.

'Shenanigans', replied the Doctor with a gleam in his eye. 'And dark forces', he added.

'Oh great! When do we get there?' Amy sighed, her tone indicating it was anything but great. 'And will there be shops?

'I Just have to throw the Temporal Co-ordinate Lockdown Switch over there' he gestured vaguely to the other side of the console, 'and no, no shops. Not even a Woolworths….ah Pick n Mix! Could anyone else go for some Jelly Ba…'

Suddenly the inside of the TARDIS lurched violently to the side, a piecing screeching grinding noise wailed throughout the room, and Amy was thrown to the floor. Her stomach dropped as if she were in a falling lift as, with a heavy thump, the TARDIS landed with a bang and everything went deadly silent. Amy grasped the console with both hands and pulled herself back up to standing.

'Nice landing Mr Bus Driver.' She shot the Doctor a filthy look.

The Doctor was frowning at the hanging screen at the rotating clockwork symbols that were dancing and spinning in front of his face.

'Time travel', he muttered to himself.

'Yes. Duh! I know. You just said', concurred Amy. 'You would think *you* would be used to *that* by now. So why the rubbish landing hmm?' The Doctor frowned at her.

'That wasn't me Amy. Something... external caused the TARDIS to slip a gear on landing and I'm not happy about it. Do you have any idea what that can do to a temporal clutch?'

Amy didn't know what that could do to a temporal clutch, and nor did she have the chance to ask either, as the Doctor marched past her towards the TARDIS doors. 'Come along Ponds. Someone has got some explaining to do. Ding-Ding! End of the line! Everybody off!' He opened the door and strode out. Rory reappeared behind Amy as she made to follow the Doctor.

'I don't suppose you know what that crash landing was about?' he asked, though without much hope in his voice.

'Nope', she replied grabbing his arm and dragging him out the door. 'Come on'

They filed out of the TARDIS and nearly walked straight into the back of the Doctor, who was stood, hands on hips, in front of a large featureless gun-metal grey door. He called out,

'Hello! Open up in there. I know what you're up to and it will have to stop if I don't like it! Hello!' He banged on the door with a clenched left fist, whilst reaching inside his jacket pocket with the other hand.

The TARDIS had materialised in what appeared to be some kind of waiting room. There was a row of three white leather chairs with chrome legs to the left of the blue police box and to the right some kind of unkempt potted plant that looked like even a good watering wouldn't save it from the compost heap. Next to that was a small water cooler that was up lit from within by a bright neon blue bulb. The water cooler gurgled at them. The Doctor looked at it briefly for a second in case it was a life form attempting to communicate. He bent his head next to it as if listening, then straightened back up, dismissing it from his mind and refocussing on the imposing door in front of them. Amy wandered over to look at an official looking notice board on the wall next to the TARDIS, while Rory went to stand next to the Doctor. The TARDIS itself was parked in front of an airlock door, that went largely un noticed by the three visitors.

Without removing his gaze from the large door ahead of him, the Doctor put a friendly arm around Rory's shoulders and said in a low voice so as not to be heard by Amy behind them,

'Rory, Can I ask you something?'

'Err yes...Sure... probably', Rory replied with the air of a man that felt he had just been asked to jump off of a tall building. The Doctor pulled out his Sonic Screwdriver and flicked it up, catching it again as it span back into his palm.

'Rory, do you sometimes get the feeling that...well, that you have become too reliant on using the Sonic Screwdriver to solve all your problems lately?'

'I don't own a Son....' , Rory began. The Doctor kept talking over him,

'Rhetorical question Rory. Rhetorical. What I mean is this. Take this large metal door for example. I could get past this door without using it. The Sonic I mean. You do know that? I have thought of at least twenty-seven ways just by standing here talking to you now. Twenty-eight actually if you were no longer breathing and I grabbed some Bio-Neuro jump leads from the TARDIS.'

'Err...ok?' Rory offered.

'It's just that the Sonic is, without doubt, the quickest option. Time is money isn't it?...well no, ok, actually it isn't in this particular case, but you take my point? I don't want to give....*people*', he gently nodded pointedly towards his flame haired companion behind them, '...the idea that I'm just a single trick diminutive equine quadruped. You do understand right?' The Doctor looked over his shoulder at Amy. Rory looked back as well, at his wife who was studying the wall intently.

'No...I mean yes... of course not', Rory agreed slowly. As usual he was on the "High Road" side of the conversation and everyone was going to get there before him.

'Good. As long as it is absolutely clear I didn't have to do it *this* way'. The Doctor gave a small cough and surreptitiously activated the Sonic. The metal door in front of them began to rise.

Rory held back as the Doctor strode forward, pocketing his device, as Amy came alongside him. 'Sonic again?" she whispered to him.

'Oh yes', he replied with a wink as they hurried up to match pace with the advancing Time Lord.

The rectangular corridor was almost completely white, with glossy black framed panels of white opaque glass at intervals along its length. A fluorescent friendly green strip of light lined the walls either side at waist height and they cast an ethereal glow on the white tiled floor.

'So this is the Newman Phillips Institute is it?' Amy declared, feigning an impressed look 'Very nice.'

'Pardon?' replied the Doctor and Rory in one voice.

'Oh you know The Newman Phillips Institute', Amy repeated. 'The foremost research facility for temporal transportation research. Situated on the dark side of Phobos in the year Twenty One Twenty Five' she continued with an air of smugness.

'And you know this how exactly?' said Rory, feeling once again that life's party was all just going on in the next room, and he was stuck in the kitchen...with the weird Uncle.

'She just read it on the notice board as we came in Rory, do try and keep up' answered the Doctor. Amy looked crestfallen and scowled at him. The Doctor laughed. On the glass panels as they passed were pictures of what looked like astronauts, all shaking hands with an elderly man in a black suit and tie. Rory read the first one out loud, a picture of a tall dark skinned man, happily shaking hands with the black suited gentleman.

'Johbar: 2114 to 1935', he moved on to the next one and read again, 'Noeclar; 2114 to 1867'. This one was under a picture of a ginger haired bearded man, also grinning inanely at the photographer. 'Happy bunch aren't they? Are they Employees of the Month do you reckon?'

'I doubt it ', grumbled the Doctor.

They were halfway down the corridor, when suddenly all the green lights turned orange and a siren could be heard somewhere off in the distance. The Doctor stopped and looked at a reading on his sonic screwdriver which had appeared in his hand once again. Rory coughed pointedly, but the Doctor ignored him.

'Time travel' he muttered again, then looked up at the ceiling and closed his eyes. Almost to himself he said aloud, 'Do you know, there was once a time, many lifetimes ago, when I would have been sent to places like this by my people, with the express instruction of shutting it all down? It's Kartz and Reimer All over again. Hah!' He looked almost melancholic as he opened his eyes and looked down at his hand, scratching at an invisible blemish on the soft black grip of his screwdriver. 'Now though...do I still have that remit? Do I still have the right to interfere? Did I ever? I mean who would know now? I wasn't *sent* this time. Nobody's left to send me anymore...' His voice tailed off as if he was now somewhere else. Some place very far away. Amy and Rory looked at each other blankly and Amy shrugged.

'Doctor?' she said with concern. Suddenly a computerised voice came over some concealed public address system.

"*Reminder Warning. Temporal Launch Imminent. Warning. Temporal Launch Imminent. All
Ancillary Time Activities Suspended Until Launch Completed. Thank you.*"

The Doctor's eyes snapped open.

'Time activities suspended? A Time Clamp!' he exclaimed. 'That's why we landed with a bump Pond. Ha! Not my bus driving. They've clamped my TARDIS. The nerve! Right. We'll see about that. Come on you two.' The Doctor turned and marched back past them, back to the open metal door and the blue box beyond. Amy was fastest to react and followed straight away, while Rory stood looking bewildered.

'Clamped?' You mean like wheel clamped?' he said

'Come ON Rory!' called Amy over her shoulder running to catch up with the disappearing Time Lord.

Rory sighed, 'Coming' he yelled and began to jog after them.

The once previously open door that they had entered though was slowly beginning to close again.

The Doctor's pace quickened as the imposing metal door began to descend. He talked out loud as if to himself,

'I mean. I'm not a small minded man...quite the opposite in fact, but clamping? It's so...primitive...and rude frankly!' He got to the door ahead of Amy, ducking his head slightly as he ran beyond the door and disappeared into the blue box. Amy was close behind and entered the TARDIS short of breath.

'What's happening Doctor?' she said loudly, out of breath. In the distance she could hear the computer voice repeating its last message.

'We've been clamped and grounded by whatever is controlling that time travel facility back there. But don't worry, now I know what they have done I can easily get around it. All I need to do is...' he span a wheel on the console, 'release the Inertial Dampeners, and switch the TARDIS Dimensional Stabilisers over there to ....'

Amy didn't hear the rest of the sentence. She had turned her back on the Time Lord to check on Rory but only managed to catch his panicked eyes as the imperious metal door quickened its descent and slammed shut with a dull thud and, more significantly, with her husband on the other side.

'Rory!' she yelled running back to the TARDIS door. 'Doctor, Rory is...'

'I know. Don't worry', the Doctor replied impatiently. 'This lot of Time butchers have made up my mind. Clamping my TARDIS. How dare they? Well, Time Lords or no Time Lords. I am shutting them down'

'Can't you just sonic the door open... again?' Amy asked. The Doctor looked sheepish.

'Hmm so Rory snitched did he? Typical. No I don't need the Sonic this time. Don't panic Pond', the Doctor said calmly. 'Once I get the TARDIS released we can rematerialize on the other side of those doors. Then I shall be having some serious words with whoever is running this miserable excuse of a time facility. Just let me ....'

But the Doctor didn't finish. A detail that went largely unnoticed, as Amy had already turned to run back out of the TARDIS door to check on her husband. She didn't see the Doctor freeze momentarily, as if turned into a photograph. She didn't see his eyes glaze and his arms go momentarily rigid. She didn't see the phosphorescent blue light that shone from his face as it swept over his features. But she did hear him knock a discarded spanner from off the console as it clattered to the TARDIS floor.

Amy span back round to face the Doctor, and saw his glazed vacant expression. A long sonorous clang reverberated from somewhere deep within the time machine. The Cloister bell rang like the worst *News At Ten* headline in the universe. Fear and doubt came together to form a single word in Amy's mouth and she set it free.

'DOCTOR?'

.3.
Theme from 'Greatest American Hero' Believe it or not
Joe Scarbury
1981

Theorising that one could time travel within his own lifetime, Dr. Sam Beckett stepped into the Quantum Leap accelerator and vanished.

He awoke to find himself trapped in the past, facing mirror images that were not his own, and driven by an unknown force to change history for the better. His only guide on this journey is Al, an observer from his own time, who appears in the form of a hologram that only Sam can see and hear. And so, Dr. Beckett finds himself leaping from life to life, striving to put right what once went wrong, and hoping each time that his next leap will be the leap home.

***

Lurching forward, Sam Beckett steadied himself with both hands against the ledge in front of him, as the rushing, whooshing sound in his head subsided. Leaping always left him feeling unsteady. It felt like he was stepping from a ninety miles per hour escalator onto static ground in a single step.

He kept his eyes closed and hoped to get a few seconds grace to get his bearings before he had to make any difficult decisions...like whether to talk or not. The ground seemed to stabilise and he listened, eyes still shut. There was a strange humming noise that was mainly mechanical, but at the same time, oddly biological. He felt strange. Well, stranger than he normally felt when assuming a new body for the first time. This was different though. Eyes still closed he exhaled. Then he cringed as a voice, addressed him.

'Doctor? Are you alright?'

Not alone then, he thought. Damn! I should be *that* lucky .It was clearly a female voice. The accent? European? Damn this Swiss cheesed brain.

Memory loss was all too common after a Leap but lately he had managed to retain a lot of information about himself from Leap to Leap. This time though he felt his brain had more holes in it than normal. Doctor? Did she call me doctor? That's good isn't it? I *am* Doctor Samuel Beckett. Am I home? Sam dared to dream the impossible dream. A dream he wished for every single time he Leaped. Maybe. Was he back at the Quantum Leap Facility? Home? Again came the voice,

'Doctor? Stop messing about. This is serious'

No. Not home. It couldn't be. It didn't feel like anywhere he'd ever been before. His heart sank. But still, he thought, a Doctor. I can work with that. I am one after all. I can wing this surely? Time to get it over with, he inhaled and opened his eyes.

In front of him was the assumed counter top he had steadied himself against. No. It was certainly not a counter top. It looked like a...well it looked like a pinball machine...except it didn't. It had an odd spiky rotating, well, *thing*, and the edge seemed to extend around to either side of him around a central column. Hexagonal. The column itself in the middle seemed to bob up and down and looked like some arcane glassblower's shisha pipe. There were switches and dials and some other things Sam couldn't even begin to guess at.

Where was Al? He turned around and addressed the source of the voice. A young attractive girl with flame red hair was looking at him with a concerned puzzled look on her face and walking towards him.

'Doctor?' she said again in a lower, more worried tone of voice. Come on Al, where are you? Sam thought, looking beyond and past the girl for any sign of the short familiar man .

Al was Sam's constant. His friend in the real world. His presence tethered Sam to reality. Al took various lengths of time after a Leap to materialise with Sam in the form of a hologram. His intel was vital however and he relied on his friend's guidance, especially in these first few, vulnerable minutes. He remembered with a sinking feeling in the pit of his new stomach that it wasn't always immediate that Al joined him. Sometimes it had even been days before Al had shown up. Sometimes it was days even for Al . Al lived his life in between Sam's Leaps. It may seem like Sam had one adventure after another from his point of view, but for Al, it wasn't like that, he could go home to his girlfriend Tina, or on occasions, somebody else's girlfriend. Gradually the initial confidence boost of knowing he had Leaped into a doctor evaporated as he took in the rest of his seemingly alien surroundings. Right, start again Sam. Take stock.

He was in a room. Good. Next. The two of them were standing on a raised, opaque floor with stairs running off in a few directions at various points. The walls seemed to glow with a soft orange light. Again he was aware of the humming. No, not humming. It was almost a gentle… pulsing? Was that the right word? A pulse suggested something alive.

Sam had honed his cold reading skills over the last few years and could generally bluff his way through the first few awkward minutes of a Leap these days, but he was at a total loss getting anything at all from his surroundings this time. He was aware again of the girl staring at him. He tried to cold read her. 'Err', he offered feebly, inviting her to give up some more clues.

She was wearing a crimson red and black checked, long sleeved top with one of the shortest black mini-skirts Sam had seen in many Leaps. Worryingly, she was also mainly wearing an increasingly hostile looking expression, more so than she had previously displayed before.

'Well?' she demanded.

'I, err…..Hi?' he fished hopefully. Floundering slightly.

Her reply, if there was one, was lost as the floor seemed to shift alarmingly under his feet and they were both thrust to the left, and then violently thrown to the right. Sam stumbled back to the eclectically adorned console in the centre of the room. Suddenly the throbbing was accentuated with the distant sound of what seemed to be a warning alarm. Sam was reeling. Where the hell was Al? He looked up at the girl and her eyes widened at the panicked expression that was all too apparent on Sam's own face. Clearly he was meant to be the one in control here. He realised that his hand had brushed against the rotating spikey looking object in front of him. He immediately snatched his hand back and the room immediately stopped shaking and returned to, for want of a better word, normal.

He was briefly reminded of a past Leap. He had assumed the identity of "Future Boy", a fictional TV character in a kid's sci-fi show called Captain Galaxy. Worth a try he thought and yelled 'Cut!' It didn't have the effect he had hoped for. There was no Director. This was no television show, which meant that this was...real? The girl replied,

'Cut? Doctor, you are scaring me. Are you cut? Are you hurt? What's happening?'

You're scared? thought Sam. I'm way ahead of you darling. Suddenly Sam had a small revelation. Scottish! Her accent was Scottish! Sam then cursed the retrieval of this nugget of information at precisely the time when it was of no practical use to him whatsoever. He clutched at this piece of floating metaphorical driftwood and went for it anyway. He said,

'You're Scottish.' Again, this only seemed to make things worse. The girl replied,

'Are you trying to be funny?' Sam closed his eyes again. Where... and who the hell was he? His sweating palm slipped forward on the console again and the floor lurched a second time. He threw back his head and gasped,

'Oh Boy!'

.4.
Just The Two Of Us
Grover Washington Jnr
1981

Rear Admiral Upper Half Albert Calavicci was having a bad day. Walking out of the "Waiting Room" area of the Project Facility he made his way over to the water cooler and pulled himself a cup of water. Taking a sip, he instantly realised it was neither what he wanted or what he needed. He abandoned the cup and went looking for a strong cup of coffee. Finding the coffee jug empty and cursing Gooshie, the Project Programmer, under his breath, he sat down heavily in a chair and patted his jacket for a cigar that he knew he wouldn't even be allowed to smoke. But just chewing on the Cuban would help though. Help him make sense of this Leap. He contemplated the last half hour.

Sam had Leaped. That much they knew. Usually Ziggy, the Project's Artificial Intelligence computer, would take no more than a couple of minutes to locate him in the midst of the intertwined knot of known histories. But this time it was different. She or more accurately He (Long story), couldn't locate Sam at all. Technically Ziggy was a He, but thanks to some input from Tina, the programmer and Al's current girlfriend, Ziggy spoke with a female voice. Whatever the gender, Ziggy couldn't locate Sam.

Usually when this happened it meant Ziggy had blown a capacitor or fried a gauge circuit or something, and Gooshie would be dispatched to patch her up. But Gooshie was adamant that Ziggy was operating to one hundred percent capacity and one hundred percent efficiency. So where did that leave them? More importantly where did it leave Sam?

Then, of course, there was the current occupant of the "Waiting Room". Al still didn't fully understand the science. Privately he suspected none of them on Project Quantum Leap fully did either. Except Sam of course, but then he did design the thing. Experience however, had given Al a rudimentary working knowledge of the theory at least. It went like this.

When Sam threw himself into the Quantum Leap Accelerator his mind got thrown back into the past of his own lifetime and he became for want of a better word, another person. His physical body stayed behind here at the Quantum Leap Facility, however the person that Sam's mind replaced got their mind shunted back here into Sam's body. It was a swap. Physically Sam's body had never left the Facility, but everything that made him Sam Beckett left the building months and months ago. Sam's mind in their body and their mind in Sam's. That was how Al understood it.

Generally the person that got switched went through a range of reactions. From the catatonic, who refused to accept what their eyes were seeing and therefore shut down their mental faculties, through to the confused and the just plain terrified.

To a degree it was quite fortunate that most of their short term memories got Swiss-cheesed on arrival as it was then a fairly easy task to calm them down and, in some cases, sedate them, long enough for Ziggy to work out just what Sam needed to resolve before he could Leap off to the next adventure. Then the poor unfortunate individual in the Waiting Room could snap back into their rightful place. Confused but generally in a better state than before Sam had helped them.

The man currently in Sam's body in the Waiting room however was…different. He was unusually lucid for a new arrival for one thing, albeit incredibly erratic and in Al's opinion, borderline insane. Al placed the unlit cigar between his teeth and replayed the last half hour over in his head while he waited for an update from Gooshie.

Half an hour earlier…

Al had paused to observe the man before speaking to him. The new arrival was sat on the white and clear Perspex table in the Waiting Room. They purposefully kept the room free of any kind of mirror or reflective surface , as the shock on the Leaper upon seeing Sam Beckett's face staring back at them instead of their own, was usually too much for them in their already fragile state of mind. Just a white floor, the table and plain blue walls.

In spite of this, the man on the table clearly seemed to know that his face wasn't quite right. He was prodding and kneading at it like a ball of pizza dough. Al observed him for a few seconds more while the man tried in vain to look at his own hair by tugging it down to eye level over his forehead. He was dressed exactly how Sam had been dressed when he stepped into the Accelerator that fateful day. A functional, if not exactly flattering, white all-in-one jump suit. A Fermi Suit Sam called it. The stranger didn't seem happy with the outfit at all.

The man, with his back to Al, paused in his examinations, as if sensing the silent sliding door opening and Al watching him. Without looking round he spoke,

'Well that was a surprise I must say. I wasn't expecting a regeneration quite so soon. Such a shame. I hadn't really had time to run the last one in properly. Odd though. There was no obvious reason to regenerate…though memory loss isn't uncommon I suppose. Odd voice'

Al was taken aback by the stranger's lucidity. Normally he was lucky if he could get more than a groan out of them. The stranger suddenly rolled off the table and onto the floor with a thump, clutching at his chest. Al ran over to him and knelt down beside him.

'Take it easy pal. Take it easy. You're safe here, nobody's gonna hurt ya. Are you in pain?'

Pain was also a new one. The Leaping process was unsettling but never physically discomforting. The stranger opened one eye and spoke,

'There's a problem with the regeneration process. Only... one heart... is working...I need...I need...' , the stranger stopped clutching at his chest and sat bolt upright, all trace of pain vanished in an instant, 'I need an explanation.' He turned to look at Al. 'I should be in pain, but I'm not. Why? I only have one heart working. Why?'

Al gawped at him. Words were his field or expertise, and flannel was his major, but he didn't know how to respond. The stranger continued, 'Only one of my hearts is working but it feels eurgh! ....normal'. The man looked revolted as he said the word normal, as if it was a dirty word. 'Here. Feel.' He grabbed Al's arm and pulled his hand towards his chest. Just as suddenly he let go of Al's arm. 'Mirror' he demanded, holding out a hand and snapping the fingers of the other.

Al snapped back to life, 'Ah, now that's not a good idea pal, y'see. You may find it a bit... overwhelming.'

'Oh, I think you will find I have an extraordinary capacity for *whelm* .Mirror. Now please'

Al found himself reaching into his coat pocket for the small mirrored cigar case he kept in there. Something about the authority in the man's voice made him want to obey without question. Maybe it was the U.S Naval training. Respect authority. Don't question. Just do. The man snatched the cigar case, opened it and began to examine his reflection. He seemed to make a mental decision and snapped the case shut, flinging it back at Al who nearly fumbled it. The man got to his feet and turned to face the wall with his back to Al. He muttered something about it "not being a regeneration after all". The man made a steeple of his fingers then turned slowly back round to face the bemused Al.

'Two questions for you Mr Calavicci', he began. 'One. Where am I? And two, where is my TARDIS?'

'How did you know my name?' spluttered Al. He was not used to being on the ignorant side of these Waiting Room conversations.

'It's engraved on the cigar case,' chipped the man, 'You really ought to give those up you know. I keep trying to tell that to Churchill, but the old dear never listens. My question's now please. And hurry up, I have a feeling that something clever is happening here without my permission. Oh and what on Androzani Major is this that I am wearing!?'

'It's a Fermi suit. Named after…'

'Named after Enrico Fermi? Particle scientist, Quantum theorist and a devil for a glass of Merlot I can tell you. Well that's one more thing I will have to have words with him about when I get round to seeing him again. That and that atomic bomb nonsense. Can I just say, this outfit is… rubbish.'

Al pulled out his multi-coloured hand-link communicator, tapped in a few commands and yelled to the ceiling, 'Gooshie, what the hell is happening here?'

The man in Sam Beckett's body raised his eyebrows and smiled. Eyes wide.

'Ooh, What's a Gooshie?'

Al ignored him, frantically tapping away. He looked at the display, frowned and then looked up at the man. Choosing to forego protocol in this instance he asked,

'Look fella, just tell me your name and what year *you* think this is and we'll get you back to where you came from'. That was all Al could think of saying. Normally he would be ready with a myriad of colourful explanations and … well, let's face it, lies to explain why the new arrival was feeling the way he was, but he was running out of patience and they needed help to locate Sam. The man grinned back at him.

'Ok fine. Hello. I'm The Doctor. And as for what time *I* think it is? Well. I think you'd better sit down.'

.5.
One Of Us
ABBA
1981

Temporanaut 245 2nd Class, Designation Hitac ran at full pelt down the corridor as the warning klaxons sounded all around her. Her outstretched hand already out in front of her ready to be read by the palm scanner at the awaiting doorway. The door parted swiftly and she passed through with little loss to her speed. The thick baggy material of her white protection suit was uncomfortable to run in but the adrenaline helped smooth her progress down the facility's tunnels.

One more corridor to go and then she would be at a crossroads. Both a physical crossroads and a moral one. And once there she would have to make her decision. She ran towards the penultimate door, hand stretched out again. As the door opened and she sped through it, her stomach lurched. There shouldn't be anyone else here. Not now. All the same though, there was a figure at the far end of the corridor, with their back to her. They appeared to be banging on the door with clenched fists and yelling. Hi-Tack was already running too fast to be able to slow down in any way close to silently, and her footfalls clattered down the echoing corridor. The stranger turned at the sound.

He wasn't wearing the usual facility uniform, and civilian visitors hadn't been allowed here since the facility was inaugurated. Hitac slowed to a walk and advanced on the man. Whomever he was she was damned if he was going to prevent her from carrying out her plan. Whichever plan she was going to eventually choose that is. She balled her hands into adrenaline fuelled fists just in case.

He was wearing a mustard yellow casual shirt under a padded sleeveless jacket and what looked like denim jeans. Hitac hadn't seen denim jeans in years. She briefly wondered if one of the Launches had malfunctioned again and thrown back an oddity from the past, but she dismissed this straight away as any throwbacks would have been contained in the Terminal area and immediately *Swept* and relocated. As she got closer, she relaxed her clenched fists as she saw the look of bewildered desperation on his face. Whoever he was, he certainly wasn't there to stop her. Hitac took the initiative,

'You there! Stand where you are and don't move' she said with authority. To her surprise, the stranger raised both his arms as if surrendering. Feigning anger was somewhat trickier when she couldn't suppress a laugh. She slowed to a stop as she got to within six feet of him. 'Put your hands down you idiot. Who are you?'

'Err my name is Rory. I..err shouldn't be here', the stranger stammered apologetically.

'Damn right you shouldn't. How did you get here?' Hitac said, looking behind her. It wouldn't be long before she was missed. She didn't have time for this. Before Rory could answer, the ground trembled under their feet and a few seconds later a muffled boom sounded way off in the distance. Hi-Tack swore under her breath, 'Davten was right, it did feedback.' She pushed Rory aside and placed he hand on the palm reader. The door didn't move. Hitac cursed again, 'Lock down and sealed'. Well that took one decision away from her then. Only one way to go now. She looked at the man next to her but he spoke before she could,

'I need to get to the other side of that door. Can you help me?' he asked her. There was such a genuine pleading look in his eyes that Hi-Tack immediately empathised with him, but there was also a strength of purpose that seemed to say, even if I wait here for a thousand years, I am getting through that door.

Suddenly the ground shook beneath their feet and a muffled boom resonated through the walls and the floors. Rory and Hitac clutched the sides of their heads as both sets of their respective ears popped as if they were on board a rapidly descending plane. Hitac recovered first and grabbed Rory by the arm.

Come with me now or you will lose everything.' A warning klaxon sounded and all of the orange wall lights turned a vibrant red. The woman cursed as the computerised voice came over the air again.

'Warning. Warning . Temporal Containment Breached. Facility Lockdown Initiated. McGregor Protocol Initiated'

'I need to get to the other side of that door' Rory repeated

'You and me both mate. But it won't open now', she said. 'Nothing will open it now until the Sweep has been completed.

She reached into a hidden pocket in her baggy suit and fished out a small metallic rectangular card with an elaborate and complex shape cut out of one end. She inserted it into a hidden crack in the wall to the left of Rory and a whole section of wall popped open to reveal a dark square tunnel. 'Thank you Davten' she whispered under her breath as she gently pushed past Rory and crouched down to enter the dark space beyond the open wall. She turned to Rory and said, 'Seriously, you need to come with me. Security will be coming soon and I can't risk you ratting me out. Besides, your only hope of surviving this is by coming with me now.'

'I'm not going anywhere. Sorry. I have to get through this door to Amy' Hitac straightened up as Rory, stuck out his jaw resolutely.

Hitac punched it. Hard.

'Sorry Rory,' she muttered as he slumped to the floor, out cold. She shook her stinging hand and rubbed the knuckles vigorously. 'You seem nice but this really is for your own good.' She looked up at the far end of the corridor one last time, before dragging the unconscious Rory into the hatch and closing it shut behind her. The door fitting so perfectly into the wall, to the untrained eye, it was never there. As the door clicked shut, so a dim line of concealed strip lights activated and allowed Hitac to see her way through the metal air conditioning service duct. She removed and unfolded scrap of paper that she had been given by Davten half an hour before. Drawn on it was a crude schematic of the Facility's layout, with a dotted line denoting the shaft she and her new unexpected companion were in. 'Launch Bay Seven is the one we are after Rory,' she muttered the comatose man beside her. 'Glad I had my Carb-o-Shake this morning', she grunted as she heaved Rory along the narrow shaft by the collar of his jacket.

Forty minutes earlier she had been sat with Davten in his quarters. He had taken her under his wing when she had first joined from the Academy. I think he had seen a kindred spirit in her. Like him, she hadn't joined up for the money. As a girl she had dreamt of adventure. Her parents had been part of the space exploration program and were rarely at home as she grew up. She would sit with her grandfather and look up at the stars, wondering where her parents were that night. Which point of light were they looking at from a vantage much closer than her. She wanted to be just like them. Adventure was in her blood and she was determined to sign up as soon as she could.

But she failed the entrance exam. Failed it quite spectacularly in fact. Her parents said it didn't matter, and that they were proud. blah blah blah. Hitac wanted adventure. There was precious little of that left to be had on Earth though. She read history books about the good old days. The days where there were still undiscovered places on the planet to explore. Frontiers. But it seemed that life had mundanity mapped out for her. A teaching position or heaven forbid, a desk job.

Then her Grandfather told her about this place. He wasn't supposed to know, but he had connections from his earlier life. The Newman Phillips Time Travel Facility. Time travel! Who knew? There had been rumours of course, but the governments were always quick to quash them. Time travel is an impossibility, they said. Proven fact, they said. Bollocks, her Grandfather had said. He knew. He had seen it for himself so he had claimed. Worked as a young man at the original installation in Arizona. He had got her into the training program on Earth. Pulled in a few favours and old debts he had told her. She remembered hugging him so tightly when she got accepted.

She had been here three years and had been on over a dozen successful missions. Successful in that she could recall each and every one of them. The failures got erased from your memory she knew, and so far she had kept hers. She stored them like precious treasure in her mind. Oh the places she had been, the eras she had visited.

She had travelled with Cook as he discovered Australia in 1770. She had watched Isaac Newton lecture at the Royal Society in 1699. She had danced in the crowd at Live Aid in 1985. She had drunk tea in Boston in 1773, watching as the United States of America took its first few steps towards independence; and she had also been there in 2055 when President Barrowman signed the papers re-absorbing them back into the New British Empire.

But then it all went wrong. Davten had discovered in the last 48 hours that the memory sweeps were malfunctioning. They were erasing memories that they shouldn't have been and worse still, they were removing and altering basic brain functions. Davten predicted that in just four or five more missions, two thirds of all the active Temporanauts would be, to all intents and purposes, lobotomised. But then twenty four hours later, even that seemed irrelevant. He had subsequently detected that something was fatally wrong in the facility's temporal energy core. Davten predicted a feedback event that would effectively destroy them all. She thought back to the conversation,

'Hitac, have you got a minute?' Davten called to her as she passed by his quarters. She smiled at her old friend and went inside. The room was barely furnished, as were all of the Temporanaut habitation cells. A bed, a small table and chair in front of a computer terminal. A few laser images of family and friends and a door that led to a solar shower and viciously efficient toilet installation. He pulled out the chair for her as he sat on the corner of the bed.

'What is it Davten? You look upset'

'Hitac. Do you trust me?'

'Of course I trust you. What is it? You're scaring me'

'This is something to be scared about I'm afraid my friend. I've got every reason to believe that the McGregor Protocol is going activate facility wide in less than thirty minutes.'

'What? How? Why?'

'Something is wrong somewhere in the Temporal Storage banks and I think...no, I know it's going to fail. Fatally feedback into the system and cause a complete shut down.'

'But if that happens we will all have our entire memories wiped. Wiped to back when we first joined up', she replied in alarm. The McGregor Sweep was the last resort. If anything happened that could compromise the Facility, this final Sweep would erase all staff memories back to day one and the institute back on Earth would send a collection shuttle to round them all back and take them back. Rumour had it that they wouldn't be treated too kindly once they got back either. Some hushed whispers talked of "disappearances"....fatal disappearances.

'Worse. With the faults appearing in the sweeps, I have every reason to believe the Facility wide Sweep will erase everything.'

'What do you mean everything?'

'Just that. Everything. Every memory you have ever had since birth' Hitac sat back and looked at Davten incredulously. 'What can we do?' she said quietly.

There was no question of not believing him. Davten knew what he was talking about. It was a commonly known secret among certain trusted members of the Temporanaut team that Davten's computer prowess had allowed him to hack into the Facility's main frame undetected. He had secured them many perks over the years and was able to alter pre-determined Time missions at the request of the Temporanauts themselves. If they had some when they had always wanted to visit, Davten could surreptitiously alter the mission to make it happen. The favours were a by-product of his real intent though.

Davten was in a similar position to her in that he desperately wanted to be part of the Technician team here at the Facility but he had been vetoed by someone high up in the organisation. Davten had maintained it was because of his left wing views when he was at University, that he was prevented from being accepted. However he didn't take no for an answer and had managed to find a loophole that allowed him on to the Temporanaut program instead. From here he could observe and secretly contribute to the experiments without them knowing. The actual physical Time missions he went on, he seemed to treat as mild inconveniences. He sat back and looked at her carefully before replying to her question.

'We can't do anything. You, however can escape'. Hitac laughed.

'No I can't. None of us can. If the facility is in Lockdown, nobody can leave. We wont even be able to leave the Recreational wing. All the doors will seal.'

'I know, but you can. With this' He handed her a small piece of metal. It was the tool she would use later. 'This will open up a service hatch that will gain you access to the air conditioning vents.' He handed her a piece of paper. 'and this map will lead you to Launch Bay Seven. Take a Pod and go'

'Go where?'

'Anywhere you want. Just go and go now. Before the lockdown. I have hacked a bit of code into the system that will let your palm scan open the doors to the main entrance door. The security hatch is by the main bulkhead doors'

'Will my palm open the main door?'

'Yes, why?'

'Because if I can get to the outer airlock, I might be able to contact Earth and get help'

'Don't! They won't help you. We don't exist remember. The whole point of the McGregor Protocol was to keep us a secret. If anything went wrong, there would be no witnesses because nobody would remember anything. Perfect deniability. If you contacted Earth they would send a ship up only to kill you. Those rumours were true...which reminds me, when you escape, don't go back to the Academy on Earth. Go anywhere else, and any*when* else, in the past. The past remember that. This is important. When there is no Facility. No institute. Otherwise they will find you. Hide. Promise me, you will hide.' If you take any word back with you in your mind, then make it Hide.' Hitac nodded.

'But what about you? What about the others? Surely you can hack into the system. Prevent the feedback?' She felt her eyes dampen and she sniffed the tears back.

'Even I can't hack into that part of the mainframe. I can make subtle changes to the peripheral sub-routines but I can't get that deep. Besides, I've made my peace. I need to stay here to help your progress. Your escape. The others I cannot help. They are all self serving, greed merchants anyway. Sylmac is the only decent one out of them but he is too far gone now. The faulty sweeps have taken too much from him. I can only get one person out, and that's you. You need to survive this.'

Back in the ventilation duct Hitac shook herself back into the present. Well Davten may not have been able to save more than just her, but she had the chance to Rory here. Poor man. First day on the job and in mortal danger as soon as he steps foot through the door. Davten's sacrifice would not be wasted.

After about fifteen minutes of inching their way along the shiny metal corridor, she reached an intersection. A quick glance at the drawing in her hand for affirmation , she awkwardly positioned Rory at the top of the intersection as it sloped sharply down to the right. She spoke out loud to herself more than anything,

'Rory, they say that the more relaxed you are in an impact, the less chance you have of sustaining any serious injury. I think I read that somewhere…I hope. You are about as relaxed as you are ever going to be. Good luck', and with that she shoved the now gently snoring Rory, off down the sliding slope of the ventilation shaft. She waited to hear the muffled thwump that signalled Rory's unceremonious arrival at the end of the ride before shuffling along to the drop off point herself. She thought to herself, Well Davten, you have been spot on so far. I hope you are right about this too', and with that she launched herself after her fallen companion

.6.
Stand And Deliver
Adam & The Ants
1981

Crazy kid, Al muttered as he hit his control pad with the flat of his palm hoping to physically knock some information out of it. It gave an electronic groan in protest. All he could get out of the man in the Waiting Room was that he was called The Doctor and that he was missing a screwdriver, a bow tie and something called a Tar-Dis. Oh and some broad named Amy Pond. As for what time period this guy thought he came from…well… that was clearly impossible.

Al had managed to back out of the room and lock the sliding door while the man calling himself the Doctor was raving with his back to the bemused Admiral, about "Temporal Kidnapping" to the room in general. Well, he could damn well stay in there until they found out where Sam was Al thought. He knocked back the last slug of coffee in the Styrofoam cup and stood up to cross to the kitchen station for a badly needed refill.

'Sugar?' said the Doctor, flinging open and banging shut cupboards as if he was conducting an orchestra. He seemed to find what he was looking for and held up a small box of artificial sugar tablets, 'Aha! Hello Sweeteners!'

Al nearly spat out his cigar.

'What the…? How in Blue Blazes!?'

'You left the door unlocked Mr Calavicci' said The Doctor, answering Al's un-uttered question. He stirred the streaming cup of coffee in his hand with a spoon.

'No I did not!' snorted Al.

'Well, let's just pretend that you did. It will save time. Now drink this and then you can tell me all about it'. The Doctor handed Al a fresh cup of coffee. Out of the blue he began singing, ' ... *A partridge in a pear tree*'

Al ignored it and yelled skywards, 'Security !'

'Ah. I'm not sure they can hear you anymore' the Doctor said sheepishly and placing the hot coffee cup down on a counter top. 'I don't think your communication sensors work anymore I'm afraid. I, err... fiddled. Oh, and you might want to save these...bits for later'. The Doctor emptied a handful of fuses and disconnected switches onto the counter top next to the coffee, almost apologetically. 'Now Mr Calavicci I need to know where I am and when I am, and, just to be clear, I am eighty eight percent certain I know the answers already so I really need you to be honest with the remaining thirteen percent please. *Two Turtle Doves*'

'It's Admiral Calavicci' Al retorted automatically and slightly childishly added, 'and I think you mean twelve percent, not thirteen.' with a small degree of triumphant pedantry.

'Oh I always allow an extra one percent for surprises, Admiral' The Doctor grinned. The grin quickly became a grimace and the man screwed his face up in pain and clamped his hands to his head. 'Arrrgh!' he cried but waved Al away as the admiral approached him 'I'm ok... just a migraine I expect. *Three French Hens*'

Al was about to protest further, but inside he waved a white flag and gave in. They couldn't find Sam, and at this moment in time, this lunatic was the only lead they had. The multi-coloured Handlink communicator in Al's hand squealed like an electronic cat and Al raised his head to the ceiling contemplating the now, defunct communication system.

'I need to speak to Gooshie and I haven't got time to take you back to the Waiting Room. Come with me' he said to the Doctor, grabbing his arm.

'Certainly Admiral. Maybe this Gooshie character can fill me in'

'I'd sure like to fill you in pal', Al muttered under his breath. If he heard him, the Doctor ignored him.

'*Four Calling Birds*', the Doctor sang under his breath as he let himself be pulled along by Al.

'Christmas carols? It's flaming August', muttered Al under his.

They made their way through the Quantum Leap facility at a brisk pace. Finally reaching an escalator that snaked down into the depths of the lower levels. They ran down the moving steps like impatient commuters and arrived at a small arched doorway. A small worried looking man in a white laboratory coat was waiting for them. He had a mop of curly red hair and a thick ginger moustache and was wringing his hands whilst looking at his watch. When he saw Al approach he walked to meet him.

'Ah, Admiral. We have a serious problem. Ziggy thinks he has located Dr Beckett but he must be…malfunctioning. It's quite impossible'. Al walked past the man and through the doorway. The little man fell into step beside him and carried on talking, 'I've run three full diagnostics and Ziggy is one hundred percent operational. I just don't understand it. It's quite, quite impossible'. Al walked up to a control desk and rounded on the man.

'Gooshie, calm down. Take a deep breath ,and look over that way, away from me, before exhaling it. Then tell me where Sam is.' The

Doctor stepped forward and grabbed Gooshie's hand and pumped it enthusiastically,

'Oh, so you are the Gooshie. Lovely to meet you. *Five Golden Rings!* Ziggy is a computer yes? Can you show me how she works please? I think I can be of enormous help to you ah-ha! *Six Geese a laying'*. Gooshie recoiled slightly and squinted his left eye,

'Dr Beckett? What are you doing here?' He looked at Al and force whispered, 'Admiral, what is *he* doing out of the Waiting Room. This is highly irregular, not to mention totally against protocol...and he appears to be singing Christmas Carols.'

'Ha! Against Protocol is my middle name' said the Doctor loudly.' *Seven Swans a Swimming!'*

'And mine' agreed Al. 'Gooshie, I can't explain it but this guy calls himself the Doctor and he is incredibly "with it" for a Leaper Christmas carols notwithstanding. I mean he's unprecedented in the compos mentis department if you know what I mean? He makes no sense at the same time though, but then it's that sort of day. Doc, Gooshie is our head programmer. Now. Where. Is. Sam?'

'Nice to meet you Doctor Bec….Doctor', stammered the small man, clearly confused. He broke free of the Doctors hand shake and moved over to the control desk. A row of opaque brightly coloured Perspex boxes were arranged at intervals in front of him in the circular room. He placed his palm face down on a vivid blue box and a needle beam of light blue light shot down from above onto and through his hand. The box lit up from within. Data readouts began to play on the screens in front of Gooshie and Al looked over his shoulder taking a sharp inward whistle of breath.

'You see Admiral. THIS is the time period Ziggy thinks Dr Beckett is'

'2125?', Al said quietly.

'Clearly impossible Admiral. It has been established that a Leap can only be within the parameters of the Leaper's lifetime. This would mean Sam lives to be one hundred and seventy two!'

'Wrong actually' said the Doctor in the background, peering up at the ceiling impatiently.' *Eight Maids a Milking...*' The other two men ignored him.

'2125, well 'ain't that a kick in the butt? Kris Kringle over there says that's where he's come from too. Why can't we find Sam? Is it because he is in the future?' Al took out a fresh cigar and placed it in his mouth unlit.

'Nine Ladies Dancing....'

'That shouldn't matter Admiral. Ziggy can localise at any point along Sam's time line. The problem seems to be that Ziggy states quite categorically that Dr Beckett is not present at any co-ordinates pertaining to Planet Earth.'

'Ten Pipers..Pi...' Al had had enough

'Will you can it with the Christmas songs! It's August and hardly relevant' he shouted. Gooshie piped up from behind Al too,

'And I think you will find it's Ten Lords a Leaping next actually' The Doctor smiled.

'Not how I originally wrote it, it wasn't. It's Eleven Lords a Leaping . Or more correctly, in this case, Eleventh Lord Leaping aha! Mind you when I wrote it originally for King Pepin the Short's wedding I had it as Twelve Lords a Leaping but it has been altered a few times over the centuries... and my self -numbering system is a little, shall we say, open to interpretation. Quite surprised it got turned into a song actually. It was only meant a list of the wedding presents I brought him. I was a bit stuck for ideas you see, I mean what do you get the King who has everything? I was going to get him vouchers. That would have shortened the song considerably. Anyway I digress. Lords Leaping is the point I am wanting to make here.' The Doctor cleared his throat noisily and spoke loudly at the ceiling 'Hello Ziggy I presume? I am the Doctor. Can you talk?' A sultry female voice filled the room,

'Hello Doctor. Yes of course I can talk.'

'Oooh nice voice. If I were to ask if this was Project Quantum Leap would I be correct?'

The cigar fell out of Al's mouth and he stood mouth gaping looking at Gooshie who was mirroring his aghast expression.

'Yes Doctor, you would be correct', replied the computer voice. The Doctor looked at Al, and winked.

'I told you. Eighty eight percent remember Admiral? Eighty eight. Though it's now nearer ninety nine. But never mind. Moving on. Ziggy! Override your location parameter restrictions and perform your probability search curve based on say...oh I don't know, a solar system wide search field for me please'. The Doctor looked smugly at Gooshie and inversely locked his fingers and cracked them loudly. His expression soon looked concerned though when he saw the face of the diminutive programmer. 'What? Why are you looking at me like that? What did I do?'

'Nooo! Ziggy! Ignore that last command, you'll overload….' Gooshie began, but it was too late. Twelve more pinpoints of light shot down from the ceiling illuminating every single box in the room and the imperceptible background hum in the room rose by several octaves. The Doctor looked sheepish,

'Ah, whoops' he said quietly. Al picked up his cigar and strode over to the Doctor, prodding him in his chest.

'What did you just do pal?' he said angrily, 'and what in the name of Don Juan is going on? How do you know about Project Quantum Leap. That is highly classified information.' The Doctor looked concerned and more than a little embarrassed.

'Remember that one percent for surprises Admiral? I think on reflection, I haven't allowed quite nearly enough'. Gooshie shouted over from the control station,

'Admiral! Ziggy is overloading. He…' pointing at the Doctor, '… has taken down Ziggy's safety buffers and Ziggy is now searching the entire solar system for Sam! How did he disable those controls in the first place? Ziggy is not supposed to respond to non-Facility personnel'

The Doctor surreptitiously dropped another handful of components onto the floor and kicked them into a corner. He looked up at the blue domed, glowing installation above them that represented the computer's physical persona.

'Ziggy old girl. Is it a girl? Cancel that last instruction there's a dear'

'It's a He...it's just Tina programmed him with a female voice to suit his Barbara Streisand ego' Al interjected. Gooshie shouted back irritably,

'He can't stop the process once it has started. In any case it looks like something else is trying to connect to Ziggy. An external processor is trying to hack in'

'Ah, that will be the TARDIS trying to find me I dare say. Hello dear! Don't let her hear you call her a processor though. She can get...touchy' the Doctor straightened his white Fermi-suit awkwardly. 'Do you chaps have anything else to wear? This really isn't me. I don't suppose anyone has a Fez?'

'I don't think you understand what's happening here', Gooshie yelled exasperated, clutching his ginger hair tightly in both hands, 'Ziggy is overloading...critically. Admiral, Facility protocols mean...' Al's finished his sentence,

'Facility Protocols mean that the failsafe system will kick in and the Lotus Protocol initiate'

'Lotus Protocol? Sounds ok. Nice flower. Nice position too. Providing you have the knees for it. Very calming', chipped in the Doctor.

'Ziggy requires an astronomical amount of energy to power his probability matrix. This whole facility is built upon phenomenal power banks and generators. Nuclear power banks. The Lotus protocol was installed by Dr Beckett to shut the Facility down completely in the event of an unregulated overload.

'Oh' said the Doctor quietly

'Oh indeed. It appears the Lotus Protocol circuits have also been tampered with' glared Gooshie accusingly at the Doctor.' Which means that instead of the facility locking down safely and dispersing the nuclear energy back into the surrounding local power grid, it will now just build and build until...

'Oh, well that's just rubbish! What a ridiculous system. Health and Safety gone mad! Right gentlemen. I think you need to show me the way to Ziggy's Mainframe. I think Ziggy needs some help in dealing with my TARDIS, and I am the only one who can do it. Where is it?'

'The Parallel Prediction Vault?' replied Gooshie before Al could stop him. Al slapped his forehead in disgust at Gooshie's complete lack of protocol, 'It's deep under the facility'.

'Great. Well lead on ,MacDuff, and you can answer me a few questions on the way...do any of you have an aspirin by any chance?'

.7.
Once In A Lifetime
Talking Heads
1981

The angry Scottish girl was advancing on a bewildered Sam. She seemed to have made a decision. 'Hand it over. I'll do it myself', she said hurriedly. She reached out her hand to a bemused Sam . He looked at her blankly. 'Jacket. Inside Pocket. Now!', she barked. Sam reached into his inside pocket and pulled out a long metal object. Before he got a chance to inspect it further, the girl snatched it out of his hand and raced back out of the door. "I'll deal with you later" were her parting words. The floor at least appeared to have calmed down. Earthquakes didn't seem to be an option though in terms of cause.

Sam exhaled in relief to be alone at last. He looked around briefly to make sure he was alone before calling out, 'Al! Al, are you there?'

Nothing.

Sam sighed and straightened himself up. He looked around again at his surroundings. Above his head a display screen of sorts was suspended on a telescopic arm. He reached up and pulled it down to his eye level. Although the screen was currently blank, it was still reflective enough, to give Sam an idea of the new body he was currently inhabiting. The face looking back at him seemed quite young. A mop of brown hair topped a youthful face and an impressive square chin. He appeared to be wearing a plain brown tweed jacket with elbow patches, a dress shirt, braces, rolled up navy-blue trousers and black boots. A neat bow tie finished the picture, and Sam instinctively pulled at the ends and straightened it. He felt strangely comfortable in the attire.

He was snapped out of his reverie by an infuriated scream coming from outside. There was no other option but to get on with this, he thought. He made his way down from the absurdly adorned dais and headed towards the frosted windowed doors that the girl had exited moments earlier. He found her staring at a large metal doorway. Arms crossed and her temper clearly set on to a low simmer.

Sam took a quick look behind him and noticed he had exited from a small wooden blue box. A police box too according to the black lettering above the doorway. Before he could examine it further, the girl spoke,

'Right. Enough mucking around Doctor. Get this door open. I can't get this thing to work. Here you do it.' She lobbed the metal rod that she had snatched earlier at Sam, who was completely unprepared for the projectile. He just about managed to catch the end of it as it span towards him, but it bounced off his palm and he fumbled it. It hit the floor on its end with a clatter and the green light at the end sprang to life momentarily. Incredibly the large grey metal door began to rise slowly.

Sam picked up the device hurriedly. The girl didn't seem to notice his clumsy recovery, as she was impatiently crouching down to get under the door as soon as she was able. The metal object, felt good in his hand. It had a comfortable weight and balance to it to it and although he didn't have the first clue what it was or how to use it, it felt somehow reassuring that it was back in his possession. He stowed it back inside his jacket pocket, noting that there was what felt like a wallet in there too. Hallelujah! He eagerly fished it out, figuring that there ought to be some kind of identification in there that would help.

The girl had disappeared under the now open door. A foreboding red light emanated from beyond it. He pulled out the leather wallet and flicked it open. To his dismay it only contained a blank square of white paper. He was about to flip it closed when, slowly, writing began to appear on the card. Sam squinted and held it closer to his face as gradually the words became clear enough to read,

   YOU ARE <u>THE</u> DOCTOR. THE 'NOT YOU ONE' IS AMELIA POND. YOU CALL HER AMY OR POND . THIS MAY NOT BE WHERE YOU WANTED TO BE, BUT IT IS PRECISELY WHERE YOU *NEED* TO BE

      -SEXY

Sam blinked as the words began to fade again. Sexy? What the hell was going on? The girl was now stood in the doorway again, glaring at him. The red light lit her from behind and coupled with the fury in her eyes, made her look like a demon freshly returned from hell.

'He's gone! Doctor, Rory's gone. Typical. Men urgh! I need to put him on a lead.' She put her hands on her hips, 'Are you coming or what?'

'I ..err yes of course' He started towards her. She put out her palm against his chest, preventing him from going further.

'Wait a minute buster. Are you ok?'

'I'm fine', Sam said, though his face betrayed anything but.

'Who are you?' she countered with a scowl. 'You are not acting like yourself. What has happened? What's your name?'

'I'm ...*The* Doctor ', Sam said less than confidently. The girl gave a laugh

'Easy. I've just called you that .Way too easy. What's my name?' she said with an element of satisfaction as if she had caught him in a trap. Sam dived in with both feet. Putting his trust in the mysterious message, he said,

'You are Amelia Pond. ' To his relief, her expression softened. It still looked mistrustful but the anger was draining. Sam decided to seize the advantage. 'I am just feeling a little out of sorts. Come on Pond, stop wasting time. Let's go and find him'. Sam has no idea who "him" was or what he meant to either her or indeed to the man Sam had leaped into and he prayed Amy didn't ask him that one next. It seemed to work though as it snapped the girl out of interrogation mode and she nodded at him.

'Alright then' she agreed though she still had a look of suspicion in her eyes. She removed her hand from his chest but not before she swiftly reached into his jacket and lifted out the device.

'I'll keep hold of this for now ok?' she said. Sam couldn't think of any reasonable excuse to disagree with her and was just relieved he seemed to have passed the first test.

They both made their way back up the red-hued corridor towards the far end, where another door awaited them. Sam noticed with concern that the first door had already closed behind them with an air of permanency. His companion didn't seem concerned. Presumably she had faith Sam could use the device again as before. Sam hoped privately he didn't have to, as recreating the earlier manoeuvre had probably already used up his quota of dumb luck for today.

'I wonder why the lights are now red' , Amy muttered. 'Red is never good'

As they approached the new door, Sam could see that it wasn't quite shut and was slightly ajar. Inserting the fingers of both hands into the small gap, Sam heaved the door across into the wall and they both stepped through.

They entered a large square room. The walls were of a similar white cladding to the corridor they had previously traversed. It was mainly empty apart for two rows of five simple white chairs that appeared to be facing a blank white wall. There didn't appear to be any other visible doors apart for the one they had just entered in from. They both looked around blankly. Suddenly two blue spotlights beamed down on them from the ceiling. Amy flinched but Sam stood stock still. A disembodied computerised female voice filled the room

'SCANNING. UNRECOGNISED INDIVIDUALS. PLEASE DO NOT BE ALARMED. WELCOME TO THE NEWMAN PHILLIPS FACILITY. IN ORDER TO PROCEED, YOU ARE REQUIRED TO VIEW THE FOLLOWING COMPANY INDUCTION. PLEASE TAKE A SEAT.'

Sam looked across at Amy who just shrugged back at him. They had a similar visitors induction presentation at Project Quantum Leap. Not that they had many visitors as it was supposedly a heavily guarded secret.

'Rory must have come this way too. Looks like we will have to sit through it', Sam said, making his way over to a seat on the front row. He wasn't about to turn down a free information presentation, especially not at this stage of his new Leap. A veritable gift horse. Amy came and sat next to him, sitting down heavily with an impatient sigh.

'Fine. But this had better not take long.' She said under her breath.

Sam was about to reply that they didn't appear to have been given a choice, when a swirling disc of black and white concentric circles appeared on the wall in front of them. The effect was mesmerising and Sam and Amy stared at it almost hypnotised. Suddenly, two hologrammatic figures appeared before them in front of swirling disc as if they had just run out of it. The disc slowly faded again from site leaving the two men stood in front of them. Both of the holograms were elderly gentlemen. One of them was wearing a formal business suit, while the other was dressed more casually underneath a long white lab coat.

The more formally dressed man on the left spoke first.

'Hello. I am Dr Douglas Phillips and this is Dr Anthony Newman. We are two of the original founders of this endeavour and we are here to applaud your decision to come to work with us here at the Institute.'

Doctor Newman took up the narrative,

'Back in 1968, we conceived and realised our theories on time travel...', Sam's ears pricked up. Time travel?! he listened intently as the man continued,'...observing that time is, in fact a static continuum we were successful in transporting ourselves back through history.'

'Though it wasn't without it's mishaps along the way', interjected a laughing Dr Phillips

Sam whispered to Amy, fascinated at what he was hearing,

'It's not a static continuum. They are nearly right but not quite. It's more like a line of string that's balled up in the middle, you can move between loops in the string...'

'Yes yes, wobbly wibbly. You've told me before' hissed back his young companion, 'Shhh!'

'Oh….right' Sam went back to listening to the two old incorporeal men in front of them. Sighing at the irony that these two were not the holograms he really needed right now.

'Indeed' agreed his hologram partner, sharing the joke. Dr Phillips continued the presentation;

'Our top secret experiments, all those years ago, have led us, and now you, to this remarkable facility. We have developed mankind's understanding of time travel exponentially. Of course we are no longer with you now in person there in 2125. We can't live forever you know. But maybe we have retired back to the nineteen hundreds?'

'As long as it's not on board the Titanic Doug', quipped Doctor Newman.' I don't relish that particular pleasure cruise again'

'Quite so' agreed his colleague with an ironic smile. Anyway, we will hand over now to this Facility's Artificial Intelligence Co-ordinator. Once again we applaud your courageous decision to work here. Pioneers of Time. Temporanauts! We salute you!'

The two holographic men froze as they stood side by side. Their bodies faded from view leaving two floating heads looking back at the audience with dead eyes. The two heads began to grow and slowly merge together until they became one singular large merged face that hung in the air in front of them. The effect was quite disturbing. An electric mesh like grid flowed over the merged face and slowly became a new one. A blank hauntingly alien face. It reminded Sam of a harlequin clown mask from the circuses that used to pitch on their family farm back in Elk ridge , Indiana from time to time. Devoid of any human characteristics, the blank faced avatar stared through them as if they weren't there. The new face then spoke,

'Welcome. I am Tic-Toc. The Controller of this facility. Named in honour of the original Project that bore the name. The Project that was the genesis of all that you see here today. As our newest recruits, you will have already completed your extensive five year training program on Earth and have been selected to have the honour of being posted here to take your place among the elite in time travel exploration.' Amy turned to Sam,

'Did you know about this place? You were only ranting the other day that humans shouldn't be messing about in time and that your people were always putting your foot down. Plus that little speech you made to yourself earlier in the corridor. We could hear you you know,' she added. Sam was reeling again. My people? On Earth? Where is here then, if not Earth?

'Amy, I can honestly say I had no idea about this. I genuinely thought I was the only person travelling through time'. That at least was the absolute truth Sam thought to himself. The Artificial Intelligence, Tic-Toc continued,

'You will now receive your Facility designate names which you will use throughout your time with us. Please remain still while the identification probe completes the scans'. Before they could protest, two red spots of light illuminated their foreheads from a source unseen in the ceiling above them. A tingling sensation, like a feather in the brain, fizzed on their foreheads.

'Identified. Amelia Pond. New designation... Ampon...Registration accepted'

'Identified. Samuel Beckett – New designation...Sambec... Registration accepted'

Sam froze. How did this computer know who he was? He looked across at Amy as the red beams disappeared. She looked at him with a raised eyebrow,

'Samuel Beckett? Seriously?' Amy laughed incredulously. 'Please don't' tell me that's your real name Doctor? After all of that mystery? Samuel seems a bit...well, ordinary'

'Of course that's not my name', he laughed nervously. 'Must be some malfunction. Before he could continue the hovering face spoke again. Ordinary name indeed he thought, irritated.

'There will now be a brief opportunity to ask any questions you may have before you will be assigned to your living quarters.' Speak' Sam opened his mouth but Amy jumped in first.

'Why do we need new names? I mean really, Ampon?' She said, turning to Sam. 'Makes me sound like a feminine hygiene product' she added in a coarse whisper. The head spoke,

'Facility rule 1.00.17 Recruit Designation. New recruits agree to forego their previous lives and given birth names, throughout their time at the Facility. Re-designation of names is part of the naturalisation process. The Sweep protocol carries the possibility that your previous lives will become redundant.' Sam spoke next,

'What is the Sweep Protocol?'

'The hologram face flickered slightly before answering'

'Facility rule 1.00.11 – The McGregor Protocol - Time travel is the most dangerous science known to the modern world. It's dangers lie not just in the physical trauma of entering the time stream, but also in the danger of exploiting the time lines to the benefit of the individual. All new recruits agree to the process of a total or partial memory wipe as and when the Facility feels that there is a danger of time exploitation and/or other uncontrolled event. The Sweep is perfectly safe and new memories will be re implanted after the process from a saved point prior to your last Time Journey.'

'I don't like the sound of that', Amy said. 'Look, I've had enough of this Doctor. We need to find my husband.' Come on. As they stood up, the voice spoke again,

'Induction Complete. Please make your way through to the habitation area, where your quarters will be assigned. Thank you Temporanauts and Welcome.'

Sam didn't know what to think. Until Al arrived he could only assume this was all real. But if he assumed that, that would mean that there was time travel that pre dated his own experiments. 1968? Why hadn't he heard about them? And that begged the further question. Why was he here and what did he have to do in order to Leap? The scope for things that had once gone wrong were immense if time travel was involved. Maybe that's why Al was taking so long. So many questions. One last one popped into his head and he voiced it.

'Tic-Toc. what year is this?'

'Environmental Query 00.001A. The year is 2125'. Sam's mind imploded. 2125? That's not possible. I shouldn't be able to travel beyond my lifetime he thought, mind racing. Unless.... He was prevented from forming the thought as he was snapped out of his theorising by Tic-Toc

'Induction Complete. Program Termination'

With a small hiss, another door had slid open from the featureless wall opposite where they had come in. Amy strode purposefully towards it.

'Amy, slow down. I wanted to ask some more questions' Sam called after her. But Amy carried on through the door with purpose and Sam hurried after. Behind him, the disembodied floating head of Tic-Toc faded away to nothing, leaving a blank white wall as before.

Walking through into the next area they found themselves in a larger octagonal room that had a small single closed doorway on each of the eight walls. In the middle of the room there was a large table with eight chairs. There was a man sat at one with his back to them. He was bent forward with his head in his hands on the table as if asleep. Next to him stood another man who was looking straight at them with red rimmed eyes and a look of fury on his face. He took one look at Amy and then at Sam.

'Hi there' Sam said, ' Err I wonder if..'

'Don't' bother' said the stranger with venom. 'You are about to die!' and with no further words and with a look of angered determination, he charged at Sam with his fists bunched.

.8.
Under Pressure
Queen & David Bowie
1981

The Parallel Prediction Vault or PPV was a subterranean, cavernous room deep under the Project facility. The raised floor was decked in metal mesh grates, through which the throbbing power core could be seen far below. It was a vertigo inducing site to the uninitiated. From wall to wall, tall cabinets full of blinking routers and digital display modules loomed like silent guardians. Glowing blue cables looped from cabinet to cabinet and at every fourth one a further thicker cable swung into the centre of the room like fluorescent buttresses, connecting to a central pyramid structure that rose to the high ceiling with its base disappearing through the floor panels and down into the core below. Interspersed throughout the main part of the room were dozens of rows of computer stations, each with a glowing monitor. Each showing a different read out. Graphs, tables, gauges and text all flashing for some attention. Normally as quiet as a library, recent events has changed the atmosphere somewhat.

Lab coat wearing technicians lurched and stumbled in all directions as the vast computer banks hissed and crackled , blowing out clouds of electrically charged smoke. The Doctor, Al and Gooshie tried to push past the stampede of scientists who were running at them in their efforts to abandon Ziggy's Parallel Prediction Vault as the hybrid computer began to lose her battle in his attempt to connect to the TARDIS Matrix.

'You'd think it would be easy to get two broads to talk to each other', muttered Al under his breath as he got shoulder barged by a fleeing scientist. 'It's getting them to stop that's normally the hard part, I remember once I was double dating two girls from the same co-ed dormitory, they had legs so long you could… '

'It's not that they're not talking Admiral,' The Doctor interrupted, 'they just can't understand each other' The Doctor paused, as a rotund man in tortoiseshell glasses barrelled towards him. The Doctor deftly sidestepped him like a matador 'Ole!' he added as if to highlight the metaphor. Gooshie wasn't so fortunate and Al picked him back up off the floor. The Doctor continued, 'If I can't configure Ziggy's probability buffers soon, the TARDIS Matrix will overload them critically and cause a Quantum Parallax'

'Yeah, English please' Al said, flinching as a computer monitor exploded close by.

The Doctor thought for a moment. 'Look, from what you've told me, Ziggy calculates Dr Beckett's position in time and space by tuning into his brainwave signature, thus finding his actual geographic location in space.' Al nodded and the Doctor continued, 'Then, by using quantum probability, she triangulates his position in Time from the fixed perspective of Ziggy himself, here in this room and at this current time, AND the brain temporal signature of whomever leaps here in Sam's place. Right?'

Al grunted his affirmation and Doctor continued further;

'Okay. Good. Well at the very same time as all that, the TARDIS is also trying to tell Ziggy where the TARDIS thinks I am,' The Doctor pointed to himself, 'based on the TARDIS's perspective, out there in the Time Vortex.' Al looked blankly at the Doctor. The Doctor sighed and extended the index fingers of both hands and drew invisible lines into each of his eyes, 'There are too many contradictory lines of sight and poor old Ziggy's data core can't cope.'

Gooshie was indignant, 'Ziggy has the capacity for a trillion floating point calculations at once, and has over 1 million gigabytes of memory', he snorted. The Doctor smiled kindly at the diminutive man in the white lab coat and patted him on the head.

'That's like a pocket calculator compared to the TARDIS.' He put an arm around the deflated man's shoulders, 'no offence and don't' feel bad, it's a very, very, good calculator,' and to Al he whispered, 'anyone got a mint? He's got breath like Aggedor's armpit'

'Tell me about it' Al concurred. Al was no scientist but he had a PHD in women. 'So what you're saying is that these two broads are laying a claim to the same man. But both of them justifying it from two different points of view and trying to convince the other one, that only they are right. And neither of them are really listening to each other?'

The Doctor thought about it, and then said 'Yes. Well no. Not really, but yes. Probably. Anyway, the upshot is...'

'Someone's gonna get their face slapped!' Al finished, he mimed a small explosion with his fingertips.

'Yes Admiral, as you say. Though if you mean this Facility being the Face, and a thermo- nuclear sized explosion being the Slap, yes indeed. I need to get to Ziggy's main control station. Where is it?'

Al grabbed a nearby fleeing scientist, 'You heard the man. Where?'

The young technician looked wildly at The Doctor in Sam Beckett's body, then looked back at Al, who glared at him.

'Over there at the back of the room Admiral Calavicci Sir' he said pointing to the rear of the room to a black console in front of a tall thin stack of blue glowing boxes. He then wrenched his arm out of

Al's grip and ran from the vault. Gooshie, who was still sulking at the criticism of his computer's capabilities said.

'I'll show you. This way'. He made off across the Vault floor.

Electricity arced viciously from data bank to data bank and there was an increasingly loud buzzing noise emanating from beneath their feet, like angry bees. The room smelled of ozone, and fear.

There were very few technicians left in the vault now. Al couldn't fault them at all. They were all simply abiding by the Facility's protocols. Some were still left at display stations though, frantically collating and rescuing downloadable data and files. They reached the main control station and the Doctor sat down theatrically on the swivel chair and interlocked his fingers. Cracking his knuckles as if he were about to perform a piano concerto. The noise increased all around them as both Ziggy and the TARDIS began the equivalent of a slanging match.

'This is getting critical', muttered the Doctor, 'Why won't this console let me in?' he slammed the keyboard in frustration then rubbed his temples with a wince of pain.

'You need to swipe your passkey card here' said Gooshie, pointing to a small slot in the side of the screen.

'I appear to have left it in my other jacket', the Doctor said sarcastically patting his pocket less jumpsuit in disdain.

'Give him yours man!' snapped Al.

'Gooshie's face paled. 'I think I must of dropped mine back there Admiral'. Al raised both his hands to the sky and groaned. The Doctor was uncharacteristically silent, which seemed to Al, was worse than the ominous buzzing whine that was building up around them. Suddenly a small square piece of plastic fell onto the desk in front of the Doctor. The Doctor looked up at the female technician that was already halfway back across the vault, running.

'Use mine', she called back

The Doctor flicked it through the slot in the screen and began to frantically type. Al, turned to Gooshie after tearing his eyes from the retreating technician's derrière.

'Who was that? I don't recognise her. I thought I knew all the honeys down here...don't tell Tina I said that.'

'She's new Admiral. Only been here a couple of days. Transferred from the UK ' he picked up the discarded passkey and read the ID. 'Employee Code OSW-11-23-1986' Gooshie answered, blowing his nose on a handkerchief and then proceeded to mop his brow with it. Revolted, Al turned his attention back to The Doctor.

'Well Doc? Are we ka-booming or what? Can you get these two gals to listen to each other? '

The Doctor looked up from the screen, though his fingers were still tapping on the keyboard as if operating independently. 'I've written a translation program and it's uploading into Ziggy's mainframe now. It's not a hundred percent perfect because your system doesn't have any Gallifreyan base code characters, but it should do the job.

Once the TARDIS makes initial contact it will rewrite my makeshift program anyway and smooth out any translation misunderstandings. Ouch!' The Doctor flinched at something on the screen, 'Sorry Ziggy, the TARDIS security protocols have just sent a warning spike. They think the old girl's being hacked…just need to add a familiarity signature to the logarithm …there we are! Hello sexy, it's only me!'

'Warning spike? Yeah ok. More like this TARDIS dame has thrown a drink in Ziggy's face' snorted Al, refusing to give up his arguing woman metaphor. 'Tina can throw a mean Manhattan I can tell you. Nearly lost an eye once dodging an olive loaded cocktail stick'

The Doctor ignored him and with a final hand flourish, tapped the last lines of base code and span round in his chair. 'Ta-dah!' he cried as the cacophony of straining computer banks slowly faded back to normal levels. 'Admiral, Ziggy should now be able to find Doctor Beckett,' and in a poor mock American accent he added 'The dames are now communicatin'…!'. He looked up at Gooshie's blank face. 'Suit yourself' he sulked. Al straightened up,

'Right. Gooshie, stay here and ask Ziggy why Sam is where he is, and what he has to do to Leap. Doctor, you come with me to the Imaging Chamber. I have a feeling I am going to need help explaining this one to Sam'. The Doctor stood up from the computer desk and awkwardly straightened his white all in one bodysuit, then massaged his temples.

'Right you are Admiral. But first we need to make a little detour … has anybody else got a headache?'

.9.
Making Your Mind Up
Bucks Fizz
1981

Consciousness rushed back in on Rory like the tide filling up an empty rock pool. He slowly opened his eyes and groaned as the bright white glare of the ceiling lights attacked his retinas. As his eyes began to get used to the light, the throbbing ache in his jaw vied for his attention. His assailant, Hitac was across the small room from him, fiddling with some loose wiring that had spilled out of the back of a white panelled computer bank. At the groan behind her she sopped what she was doing and turned to Rory. She walked towards him. She was an attractive woman, thought Rory, late twenties maybe early thirties he guessed. She had long straight brown hair that was swept back into a ponytail. Dark skin and soft kind eyes. Oh and a right hook like a featherweight boxer. She knelt down to where he was sat, up against a wall and fixed him in a stare with those friendly brown eyes.

'Hello Rory. How's the chin?' she said with a grin

'You hit me?' was all he could think of saying. She laughed.

'Yes. Sorry about that. I saved your life actually'

'But you hit me?' he repeated. Hitac rolled her eyes.

'Ok. Yes. I hit you. But look. We are alright. These two Pods are still viable. The overrides must have been damaged in the feedback event. I think I can get them to launch. We can escape the Sweep!' Rory had absolutely no idea what she was talking about.

'Err Right. Great. Do you mind telling me where we are and how I can get back to the large door please?' He slid himself up the wall until he was stood up straight. Hitac stood up level with him. Wincing as he rubbed his backside. ' Did you give me a kicking while I was down as well?'

'You really are a stranger here aren't you? You really don't know where you are? How did you get here? And no, I didn't give you a kicking. That's probably where you landed after dropping out of the ventilation shaft up there.' She pointed up at a small rectangular opening high up in the wall

'Oh. Right. That's...ok then. Look, I don't know where I am. My friends and I just arrived here. Probably by mistake. We usually do. I just need to get back to Amy. She will be missing me...or actually more likely mad at me for not being where I am supposed to be'

Hitac laughed. 'You make her sound like your wife'. She stopped laughing as she saw his expression,'...oh, ok she is your wife. Oh Rory I'm so, so sorry. If she hasn't managed to leave the Facility by now, I'm afraid you are not going to see her again'

'What are you talking about? Where is she? What's going on?'

Hitac sighed. 'The short answer is that you are on a top secret scientific research base that conducts experiments in time travel. She expected some kind of shocked look on Rory's face but she found none. ' Basically we go backwards and forwards in time and if we make any errors or pick up any information that we could exploit in the present, then the Facility's Controller wipes those memories from our heads. It's not pleasant but we...well most of us are in it for the money.'

'Right. Go on' said Rory in a level tone. Hitac was in to minds as to whether he was either poking fun at her or just an idiot, as to the layman, these revelations ought to be causing some form of consternation or at the very least, mild curiosity. Instead, Rory seemed to be taking this in his stride as if time travel were some sort of everyday occurrence for him. She also started wondering if he was in fact a spy sent from the Main Base back on Earth. She continued,

'Basically in the last few days, a colleague of mine has discovered that there is something wrong in both the memory wiping system and also the energy storage containment. He feared, and was just proved correct, that the Facility was building towards a critical feedback event. This feedback has caused a Facility wide lockdown. Nobody can get in and nobody can get out. This is in preparation for the McGregor Protocol'

'Which is?'

'Which is a Facility wide mind wipe. In normal circumstances this means wiping our entire memories from when we first joined the institute. It's a last resort to protect the secrets of the Institute. The trouble is, my colleague...my friend, believes that the problems inherent in the memory wipe system will mean that this Final memory sweep will actually wipe all of our memories from the day we were born onwards.'

'The Doctor will help' Rory said

'Who?'

'The man we travelled with. The Doctor. He can help. Whatever is wrong here. He will fix it, or rescue us all, or something. He is a bit odd but he is clever. I mean properly clever. Whatever the problem is he will sort it. I think. That's why I need to get back to the door. He was on the other side of it.'

'Rory. I'm sure your friend is as clever as you say, but he wont be able to get to you. Not now we are on lock down. Plus I doubt even he will be clever enough to stop the Sweep in time. Can you hear that?' Rory listened. Beyond the low level hum that was coming from the equipment in the room, he could here a voice counting down.

'Sweep Initiated. Effective in forty five minutes and thirty three seconds... '

'He will make it. Trust me'. For the first time Hitac detected a small degree of uncertainty in his voice

'Over there are two Time travel Pods. Those are the vehicles we use to travel through time. The Facility Lockdown ought to mean that they are deactivated, but either Davten, my friend, has managed to override the system, or more likely, judging by the damage to them, the feedback has made them viable...ish'

'Ish?'

Hitac was getting annoyed.

'Look. All my life I have wanted adventure. Something more than the everyday mundane life that most of us on Earth have to exist through. Since I joined the Facility I have experienced things you can only dream of...'

'Oh I don't know, I have...'

'Shut up! Listen. I am not going to sit here and just give up. I'm not going to let the Sweep reduce me to a walking zombie. Reset to day one. No chance. I am going to get into one of those Pods over there and escape. I don't know where to and I don't know to when, but I am going to take my chances. I have dreams I still want to live out. Davten sacrificed himself to get me to this point and I will be damned if I am going to waste the chance. There are two Pods Rory. I can tell you how to operate it. It's not that complicated really. Marty McFly stuff really, if you've ever seen that museum exhibit? I am really sorry about your wife, but the chances are her ship or whatever you arrived in, will be clamped. There will be no escape from the Sweep for her or your Doctor friend either. They will be reduced to newborns in effect. You alone have a chance to escape this'

'I'm not leaving her' Rory answered resolutely. A shower of yellow sparks from behind them made them turn round. Hitac cursed under her breath and ran over to a control panel

'It's the Safety protocols' she groaned, 'The lockdown is still trying to shut down these Pods. We have to get going'

'Hitac? That's' your name right?' Rory called back

'Sort of, yes. It is here. What is it?'

'I'm no expert on all of this...'

'No kidding' she shot back irritated,

'...but I know that equipment doesn't look safe. Just wait here with me. My friend is also a time traveller. That's how we got here. In his time machine. He will find a way to get to us I am sure. Don't use those Pods. They don't look like they will work.'

'Well that explains why you are taking all this so calmly. Apologies. I thought you were just an idiot.'

'I get that a lot' Rory agreed. 'don't worry about it'

'It doesn't matter though. Even if your friend does have a time vessel too. The Facility will have disabled it. It has a disruption field of five kilometres from base centre. He won't be able to leave either and he won't be able to get through the main doors even with a thousand megaton bomb. Yes, these Pods don't look like they are 100%, agreed. But I am willing to risk it rather than stay here.' She had prized off the back panel of the control desk and was pulling and searching through wires and couplings. It reminded Rory of Amy ploughing through a clothes rail in the January Sales.

'Hitac, he will find away. Please don't risk it. Trust me.' He said. Hitac looked up from the haystack of wires,

'Rory there are only two men I trust. My Grandfather and Davten. One is dead and the other soon may as well be. I'm going. And if you have any sense, you will go too.'

.10.
Can You Feel It
The Jacksons
1981

<<SWEEP IN 00:41:17...00:41:16...00:41:15>>

Sam operated on instinct and his body muscle memory took over. As the furious stranger got to within range, Sam leapt up a foot in the air and executed a perfect roundhouse kick that connected precisely on the man's jaw and he crumpled to a heap on the floor. Sam immediately knelt down and put him in the recovery position and straightened up, straightening his bowtie.

'Sorry, I had no choice', he said, more to himself than to anyone in particular. He looked at Amy who was staring at him wide eyed and mouth open. Sam instinctively knew he had just made a huge mistake.

'What was that?!' Amy said in disbelief

'Self defence Amy, he was coming straight at us. I don't think he's injured. He's Just out cold'. Sam explained.

'Yeah, I know he's just unconscious. I meant, what was that you just did?. You don't do that...I mean, I didn't know you could even do that...you don't do... physical'

Sam knew instantly that the roundhouse kick was a mistake. That must have been seriously out of character. He berated himself for acting so impulsively, but that was the whole point of martial arts. You did act without thinking. Especially in defence. You don't have time to think. You just act. He cleared his throat,

'I don't like doing that. It just sort of kicks in instinctively you know...no pun intended?' He hoped that weak explanation would placate her. It seemed to, though her next words confused the hell out of him.

'Right. Well. Ok then. But next time we get attacked by a Silurian or a Weeping Angel can we for once not run down the nearest corridor and use a bit of Bruce Lee instead?' Before he could respond. The man at the table spoke. Keeping his head in his hands he said,

'Sylmac was right though. You are about to die' Amy and Sam walked over to the table, and warily moved around to face the semi-prone figure. Sam slowly pulled out a chair and sat down opposite.

'Sylmac? Is that his name?', he asked quietly. The man raised his head. He was a lot older than the comatose man on the floor. He had thinning black hair that was sliding into silver at the sides of his head. He had a look of total resignation on his face and his blue eyes looked bloodshot and red rimmed like his colleague. He was dressed identically to his partner too. A white high rounded neck top under a more rigid white composite body armour.

'Yes, for now it is', the man muttered. Just as mine is Davten….for now.'

'I don't understand', Sam said 'What's going on here?'. Amy had taken the chair next to him and had quietly sat down beside Sam.

'Have you seen another man come through here? Short. Thin. Terrible dress sense. His name is Rory?' she thought for a moment before adding, ' or maybe Rowill? Rowpon?' thinking about their recent renaming ceremony from earlier. The man looked at her blankly as if noticing them for the first time. He looked at Sam and frowned.

'Who are you? Why aren't you wearing Temp Suits? New recruits should arrive fully dressed in Facility uniform' Sam looked at Amy but she just shrugged her shoulders.

'We are… visitors here' he managed.

'Nonsense! We don't get visitors here anymore. Are you here to shut us down? I warn you, if you are not, then you are trapped here. The Sweep will start soon, and we know the horrible truth of it now eh Sylmac?', He was addressing the fallen man who was sitting up and rubbing his jaw groggily. Sam began to stand up from the table, but the man called Davten motioned him to sit back down. 'Say nothing' he whispered

'What happened? Why does my head hurt'. Davten stood up and helped the man back to the table and sat him in a chair.

'You fell my friend. You had another blackout', he said gently. The man called Sylmac thumped the table in frustration.

'Again? Damn the Facility. Has the Sweep begun yet?'

'Not yet my friend. And unfortunately Head Quarters have sent up two new recruits as well. Just in time to get their minds wiped', he indicated towards the two newcomers. Sylmac looked at them, the previous blaze of anger that was in his eyes was now pure pity.

'Poor bastards…I need to lie down. Just for a little while', he stood up and made his way over to one of the doorways. He paused to a second as if remembering and turned ninety degrees to the next one. The door slid open and hissed shut behind him .

'Sleep well my friend', Davten muttered watching the door close behind his colleague. Then he turned to Sam. 'I don't know how you got here but you are doomed. I assume from your attire that you haven't been through the Temporanaut training and therefore don't know about the Sweep?'

'We were told next door that it had something to do with memory wiping' Sam said. Davten nodded

'The McGregor Protocol was in place to selectively wipe the memories of us Time travellers so that we wouldn't corrupt the time lines, only...'

'Only?'

'Only it has been corrupted itself. Each Sweep takes more and more of our memories. It's making us forget who we are. Come with me'

Davten stood up and walked over to another of the doors and it slid open. Sam and Amy followed. It was a small room with the back wall filled with computer display screens. Davten was sat at a keyboard and typed in a sequence.

On a display a series of medical charts came into view. Sam stepped forward and read them with a frown. Davten turned to Amy and said,

'Here, watch this. This is the official company line regarding the Sweep.' Amy sat down and watched a short sterile presentation about the moral responsibilities of time travel and the supposedly harmless failsafe process of selective memory wiping. Davten commented over her shoulder. 'There are fifty eight personnel here in the Facility. Fifty eight. And we are all about to be erased forever. Sam looked up?

'What do you mean? I can see from these medical records that the memory sweeps that you call them, have recently been affecting more than the areas of the brain used for short term memory, but there isn't anything actually fatal here.'

'The Final Sweep. The one you can just about hear the countdown for? Look at that screen there' The man indicated to a readout. Sam read it with growing alarm,

'But that's insane? That will wipe out all memory. Long term and short term. There will be nothing left'. Davten nodded his agreement.

'We will be left like newborn infants'

'Worse'

'What do you mean?'

'Look at these readings here. If the concentration of this memory wipe is as shown on this graph here, then there is a more than 85% chance that all base level functions of the brain will be wiped too. Davten stood by Sam and read where he was pointing,

'...Sir, you are right. I hadn't properly made that connection. It's murder' Amy joined them

'Doctor? What's he talking about?'

'Amy, once this thing activates, not only will it make everyone forget who they are, it will go further, it will also make their brains forget how to operate. Our brains will forget how to send messages to the other organs. We will forget how to breath, how to regulate heartbeats, how to control the release of chemicals. All the things our subconscious brain does for us, it will forget. Unless we can control our bodies manually, we will all die.'

'We ought to be able to do that though. Look, I want my arm to move up. It moves up.' She demonstrated by raising her right arm up and not so gently, slapping his forehead.

'Yes, that's easy for you now. That's because your brain is sending impulses to your muscles to expand and contract at just the right amount to make your arm move exactly how you want it to. Do you think you could consciously fire a neuron from your brain to the exact area in your body on command whist at the same time keeping your other muscles right where they are to stop you falling over, whilst processing the huge level of information that is coming in through your eyes and ears. Bearing in mind all the images coming in from your eyes are in fact upside down and your brain is compensating for that? Amy, our brains are performing billions of tiny calculations every single second, all without you being aware of it. Could you do that manually if you had to? It would be like plugging yourself into the internet and being expected to control all the websites all at once…on a trampoline. No trial run, no practice. Just straight away. Then there's your immune system, your temperature regulation, your food digestion…'

'All right all right, you've made your point' Amy said irritably.

'So off you go then' Sam looked at her blankly

'What?'

'Save the day, Sonic it, do something clever'

'Err…right…err' Sam stammered. Even if Al was here Sam doubted he could do anything about this.

'Look , Amy. There are some things I need to tell you…starting with this. I don't actually know what to do'

Davten put a friendly hand on his shoulder.,

'Don't beat yourself up over it. I have been studying this for years and watching these anomalies for the last few days. I pride myself that I know a great deal of what happens here, but there really isn't anything I can do to stop it. I have hopefully managed to aid at least one person off this base. If she has made it to the Launch Bay that is. I may be able to help you too if there is time. Wait here. I need to get something.' With that he left the small room and disappeared into the recreation room. Sam and Amy followed but he was too fast and had already disappeared from view to another area. Sam looked back at Amy and immediately wished he hadn't.

.11.
Going Back To My Roots
Odyssey
1981

<<SWEEP IN 00:35:35...00:35:34...00:35:33>>

Rory leant back heavily against the launch bay wall and slowly slid down to a crouch on the floor. The countdown was continuing beyond the jammed door, and although he was aware of it, he was no longer hearing it. He rubbed his temples before finally running his hands back through his hair.

Hitac crossed the short distance from the opposite wall where she was stood and crouched down in front of him.

'How can you be so sure your friends will come for you?' she said softly. 'I know this facility. I know it's protocols and I know it's fail safes. This Doctor, won't be able to get to us in time not that we have much time left anyway. We have been incredibly fortunate that this launch bay has been damaged enough to let these two pods leave and bypass the lock down. I'm sorry Rory but I'd rather take my chances in some other time than lose everything I am by staying here.' She looked at him imploringly. Rory looked up at her.

'I have to wait', he said. 'She is my wife and I have waited a long, long time for her before now. Trust me on this. I can wait again.'

'But if you stay, you will both forget each other anyway. You will forget *everything*. At least this way you will still remember. You will still be Rory'. She grasped his hands imploring him.

'But if I am not with Amy, that would be worse. I'd rather forget everything than know I have lost her forever. Do you know something Hitac? Never be happy.' She looked at him blankly

'What do you mean?'

'Because being happy is the most terrifying thing in the universe. Once you are happy, it can be taken away from you and that's terrifying. Amy makes me happy'

Hitac looked at him for a long second and saw the fear in his eyes. The absolute fear that he would lose the one thing that made him happy. She blinked as he continued suddenly,

'Anyway, there is still time. My friend will come. He may be a lot of things but he always comes through in the end. Wait here with me Hitac. Those Pods are malfunctioning. You said it yourself, you could end up anywhere. Any when! In the heart of a sun, or in the time of the dinosaurs. Give him a chance, please'

Hitac released his hands, stood up and screamed at the ceiling in frustration.

'Gah! I don't know how long these Pods will remain viable. But I do know that...', she paused to listen to the countdown, ' that in thirty two minutes and twenty seconds, the Sweep will activate and everyone left in this facility will have their entire memory wiped. Erased. There will be nothing left of them. Nothing left of who they are, or of who they were. I'm sorry Rory. I'm going to go.'

She took out a writing stylus and scribbled some notes on a piece of notebook paper and handed both paper and pen to Rory. 'These are the activation sequences for Pod Two. If you change your mind, and I hope that you do, use them to launch the Pod. The screen will ask you for a date and a time for the destination. The Pods are defaulted to go to the main facility back on Earth but you can choose *when* you arrive. If the Pods aren't too damaged that is', she added.

'I understand' said Rory standing up. He couldn't blame her. She didn't know the Doctor. She didn't know what he was capable of. Mind you, he thought, did he? Really? If he was honest, his reluctance to use the Pod was more born out of his desire not to leave Amy behind, rather than his faith in the Doctor. Who was he to persuade Hi-Tack to risk her entire existence on his word alone?

Hitac opened the oval door to Pod One and climbed into the seat. It was angrily fizzing and popping with electrical energy, and Rory could tell by the look on her face that she wasn't totally convinced that it would operate as she had hoped. But she had made her mind up. To her the risk of being flung aimlessly into the Time Vortex was still preferable to losing her mind entirely. She typed in the activation codes and looked up at Rory as the door began to swing shut.

'Rory, I've set my time co-ordinates to one hundred and fifty years in the past. If I set if for the future there is an chance that the Institute will trace me and be waiting for me . They could send me back here... or worse. My family has an estate on the Scottish moors. It's nice and remote. Somewhere to aim for anyway, once I arrive'

Rory nodded, as Hitac continued,

'I wish you well Rory Williams. I hope your friend finds a way to save you and that you will be with Amy again. Just make sure you are certain. The Sweep is total and irreversible. There is no escape from it and it is one hundred percent effective. Good bye Rory'

'Good luck Hitac. Rory had to shout because the Pod door had now sealed and no sound would penetrate. He could still see her through the small clear viewing screen built into the door panel.

Hitac smiled back that she understood, though her smile had more worry than fondness in it, and Rory could see the wetness in and around her eyes. She motioned for him to stand back from the door.

He stepped back at the far end of the Bay. The Pod began to shake and a bright blue light encapsulated it. Just as the electrical crackling became too painful to his ears, Hitac looked up sharply from an obscured display panel and shot him a look of complete and utter panic. She began to shout something.

'Hitac, What's wrong? I can't hear you' Rory mouthed to the stricken Temporanaut. Suddenly the Pod shrank away from his view into a pinpoint of light, before that too vanished and the bay was silent. Silent apart from the distant countdown outside.

Rory felt sick. What had gone wrong? What was she trying to tell him? Was the Pod *that* faulty after all? Where had she ended up, and when? He wished vehemently that she was safe wherever she was. He looked across at the identical Pod Two. He wasn't going to use it. He was sure of that. He unfolded the note that Hitac had handed to him. There was a three step series of button sequences that described how to operate the Pod, followed by a sentence,

"It is better to risk starving to death than surrender. If you give up on your dreams, whatHYPERLINK "http://www.brainyquote.com/quotes/quotes/j/jimcarrey411044.html"'HYPERLINK

"http://www.brainyquote.com/quotes/quotes/j/jimcarrey411044.html"s left?" – Thank you Rory – Hila Tacorien (Hitac) x

Rory folded the paper and put it in his pocket. Then he sat back down and listened to the diminishing countdown. Good luck Hila Tacorien. I hope you ended up somewhere safe, he thought to himself. He made a mental note that he would tell the Doctor about her. If he ever saw him again that is. Maybe he could help her.

'Come on Doctor', he muttered under his breath.' Where are you?' He looked down at the pen in his hand that Hitac had given him and then up at the bare white walls. And he wondered...

***

The Doctor and Al ran back from the Parallel Prediction Vault. Back through the endless string of corridors. Al lead the way. Surprisingly quick on his feet for an elderly cigar smoker the Doctor thought to himself. The pain in his head was getting worse and he was secretly hoping it wasn't what he thought it was, but at the same time secretly knowing that, as with most things it usually was what he thought it was. As they turned a corner at pace, the Doctor suddenly skidded to a stop outside a doorway marked LOCKERS. He looked down at his plain white jumpsuit and shuddered.

'Wait a minute Admiral. I will be thirty seconds...forty tops' . Before Al could protest, the Doctor had disappeared through the door.

'This is really not the time...' he began to say, when his hand link bleeped at him from his pocket. He fished it out and moved it back and forth in front of his yes as if trying to focus on the display. '... Interesting' he muttered and looked up the ceiling, 'Are you sure about this Ziggy? Oh right. Damn, the communication system is down'. Just then the door to the Locker are flung open and the Doctor streaked past him,

'Come on Admiral. No time for a smoke break', he shouted as his disappeared round the corner. Al did a double take and called out,

'Hey! Have you been in my wardrobe locker?' The Doctor shouted back,

'No time for that now Admiral, come on. It's fairly tricky following you to the Imaging Chamber when you are behind me!' Al, swore under his breath and ran to catch up with the mad time traveller, who was now wearing a mismatched selection of Al's wardrobe.

'I'm getting too old for this'

… # .12.

For Your Eyes Only
Sheena Easton
1981

I am Doctor Samuel Beckett. I am a time traveller. That should be mind-blowing enough, but today I have had it blown beyond the limits of my mind's capacity for wonder.

I thought I was the first. The first to realise that the possibility of time travel was within human understanding. I did it. I travelled, ok maybe not quite how I planned but I did it. Now I discover that others may have beaten me to it. Don't get me wrong, I'm not bitter. Just amazed. And if that wasn't all, I seem to have Leaped into another Time Traveller that isn't even from Earth.

It seems increasingly likely that I am on my own with this Leap. I don't blame Al, or the rest of them back at Project Quantum Leap for not being able to find me. If this really is 2125, then I have leaped way beyond my own lifetime. Way beyond my planet too it would seem.

I guess I am going to have to figure out what I am here to do myself. My money is on stopping this Sweep from erasing all these people's memories. But where do I start. I don't have enough knowledge to be able to stop this and by the sounds of it I don't have a lot of time left either. Maybe the answer lies with Amy. Maybe she knows how to fly the contraption we arrived in. Maybe I can figure out a way to rescue them by taking them out of the Sweep's range.

Of course, there is the other possibility that this Doctor did that originally and I am really here to make sure all these people do lose their minds. But that doesn't sit right. It would be condemning them to die if my interpretation of the scan results are correct.

To hell with it! Right or wrong, I can't sit by and let all these people die. Without Al and Ziggy I am shooting in the dark, but if its mu choice...and it looks like it is. I'd rather fail doing what's right, than succeed in doing something that's wrong.

I just hope that I can do whatever it is I need to do, and I have a sinking feeling I am going to have to break rule one, and tell Amy the truth of what's going on here and to hell with the consequences....

.13.
Hello Again
Neil Diamond
1981

<<SWEEP IN 00:31:59...00:31:58...00:31:57>>

'Right. Enough is enough mister! I don't care what you say, you are not the Doctor. You look like him but you are not him. What have you done with him?' Amy lifted up a piece of broken chair leg and brandished it at Sam. 'I'm warning you, I know how to take care of myself'. Sam didn't doubt it for a second.

Al still wasn't there and for the first time, Sam wasn't totally sure he would be this time. And this surely wasn't a normal Leap by any stretch. Surely the rules didn't apply anymore? He was running out of options. He was going to have to tell her the truth, and pray that she accepted it enough to help him work out why he was here. He had to tell her, but he feared her reaction. All he had said was that he didn't know what to do, and he got this reaction already.

'Tell her truth Sam!' came a familiar voice behind him. Sam nearly cried in relief as he heard his friend's voice. He turned round and immediately the panic in his stomach returned as he saw the look of worry on Al's face. 'It's ok Sam. It's ok to tell her the truth...trust me it will be a whole lot easier if you do'

'Al! I could kiss you. Where the hell have you been?'

'Sam , this is complicated and I don't have a lot of time. It's all gone a bit caca. I'm sorry it's taken me so long to find you'. Amy lowered the chair leg slightly,

'Who is Al? Who are you talking to?' she demanded. Sam ignored her.

'Ka-ka? Really? Again? Look It's ok. I've only been here about an hour. It was a bit hairy a minute or so ago but I think I...'. Al cut him off.

'An hour?. Sam, you have been off our grid for nearly twenty four hours. I don't'...' Al turned as if listening to some unseen voice. He nodded and turned back to Sam. 'Ah, apparently there has been some kind of Time distortion effect and the Doctor here has calibrated the Imaging Chamber to...' he looked over his shoulder again, ' to synchronise the...'. This time it was Sam that interrupted,

'Who is with you? Which Doctor is there? Doctor Beeks? Verbena is that you? ' Doctor Verbena Beeks was the Quantum Leap Project Psychiatrist. It might be useful to speak to her right now Sam thought. He feared he was losing his mind.

Amy tried again,

'Err hello! Doctor...Imposter...Whoever you are. I said, Who are you talking to?' Amy approached Sam who had his back to her, 'Angry girl with blunt object here! Hello!

Sam ignored her as Al continued,'

'Well, this is going to be tricky to explain Sam, but it may be easier just to show you. The Doctor says, in your jacket pocket should be a screwdri....sorry, a sonic screwdriver. Sonic? Sounds like a cocktail. Reminds me of this one night in Toledo, there was this blonde called Ruby, man she had the most fantastic...what? Yes I am getting to that. Let me handle this will ya!.', this last part again to the mystery invisible person somewhere over Al's shoulder. To Sam he continued, 'you need to calibrate the Sonic Screwdriver to setting forty seven and activate...'

'I don't have it anymore' Sam interjected.

'Whadyamean you don't have it?'

'If you are talking about a metal rod type thing with a black leather handle, a mad Scottish girl took it.' Sam hissed. Al groaned.

'Amy Pond?' he asked.

'That's her name, yes. Pretty girl. Pretty angry though. Very angry actually. She's behind me now'

'I *can* hear you, you know' Amy said

'Ask her for the Sonic Screwdriver Sam, Trust me.' Sam turned back from is friend and faced the bewildered Amy Pond

'Amy, Can I have the Sonic Screwdriver please. I promise I will explain everything' he implored her, noting with some concern the broken chair leg in her hand. Amy frowned at him for a moment, before lowering the makeshift wooden club to a less offensive position. Though not letting go of it completely, Sam noted.

'You had better' she growled, fishing the requested device out of her shirt pocket, and flinging it towards Sam. He caught it easily this time and swung back round to Al. The hologram moved round next him and pointed out the setting controls to his friend.

'That's it, setting forty seven, now press that button there'

Sam activated the unit and the green end lit up brightly with the familiar accompanying electronic buzz. The air seemed to shimmer slightly and there was a loud clatter as Amy dropped the chair leg behind him on the floor. Next to Al appeared Sam Beckett. But of course Sam knew it wasn't him, merely his body. A body and a face he hadn't seen in what felt like an eternity. He was dressed in the white Fermi suit that he wore when he stepped into the Quantum Leap Accelerator. Back when his life had made sense. Back when his life was actually *his* life.

Aside from the functional white all-in-one, his body was also appeared to be wearing a bright red fedora and a white US Navy Admirals jacket complete with honour pixels and gold buttons. It was also wearing a wide grin and it was waving at him enthusiastically. The effect was both and at the same time disconcerting and utterly ridiculous. It was compounded further when his body spoke to him in his own voice.

'Hello? Hello .Calling Doctor Beckett. Can you hear me, over? Ha-ha! Of course you can. I can see it in your eyes...my eyes. Ah, this is going to be awkward. Hello Pond! Have you missed me? Where's Roranicus?'

Sam looked imploringly at Al, who rolled his eyes.

'Sam, this is the Doctor. You may want to sit down for this one, but he's...'

'A time traveller? Yes I know. I've worked that bit out for myself' Sam replied slowly walking around the hologram doppelgänger in front on him. 'Al, I'm in the year 2125. There's has been time travel on earth since 1968!, do you know what this means?'

'Ah..err yeah. You know that already huh? Ok. Look just shush a minute.' Al turned his attention from Sam to Amy. 'So, this is Amy Pond? Wow, look at those legs...Wheeooo! Reminds me of my second wife. Did you ever meet her Sam? Legs you could ski down... or up for that matter...or was it my third wife?'

'Oi Excuse me! I can hear you, you know! Doctor, Who are these two and where did they come from?' Amy walked towards them, slightly affronted at the lasciviousness in Al's tone. Al raised his eyebrows at the Doctor who grinned back at him awkwardly,

'Ah yes, sorry Admiral. Should have mentioned, the Sonic will allow both Dr Beckett AND Amy here to see and hear us ...both' Al looked embarrassed,

'Err, right. Ok. Err sorry Miss, no offence meant I'm sure', he stammered.

'It's Mrs to you, I am a married woman and start explaining... someone!' Sam returned from his inspection of his double and walked up to Amy. He gently pulled out a chair and she lowered herself onto it on autopilot. He crouched down in front of her, taking her hands.

'Amy, I'm sorry. You are right, I am not your Doctor. I am A Doctor but not the one you think I am. That man over there is your Doctor' The man in the red had waved at her. 'There was an experiment that went a little Ka-ka....'

As Sam explained the Quantum Leap project and all that had happened before, in the distance the automated countdown continued.

Un-noticed by the group, Colbak observed the scene in the middle of the room with cold interest. He turned to his invisible advisor and said quietly,

'Why is it, wherever we seem to go, that infernal Sam Beckett turns up? Does Lothos know about this?' He listened for a moment to the reply only he could hear, 'Well go and find out you fool. The last thing we need is Beckett blundering about here complicating things...besides. I have some unfinished business with him,'

.14.

You Better, You Bet
The Who
1981

Three Days Earlier

Leap Observer Alpha Grade, Thames was having a bad day. Walking out of the "Waiting Room" area of the project facility he made his way over to the water cooler and pulled himself a cup of water. Taking a sip, he instantly realised it was neither what he wanted or what he needed. He abandoned the cup and went looking for a strong cup of Earl Grey tea. Finding the pot empty and cursing he sat down heavily in a chair and twirled his wooden handled walking cane that he didn't actually need to aid his movement. He just liked the feel of it and it went with his metallic copper shirt and brown tailor fit leisure suit with the raised ribbed shoulders. He tapped the cane impatiently on the smooth white tiled floor with vivid red marbling. He contemplated the last half hour....

Deep beneath the streets of London, unbeknownst to the inhabitants of the sprawling city, The subterranean base of operations for the organisation simply known as The Project throbbed with barely contained power. Thames strode down the main corridor towards the command hub. His walking cane clacking every third or fourth beat, betraying its use as a cosmetic affectation rather than for any physical support. The door slid open and he walked into the room. The glowing baleful globe of sparking light that represented LOTHOS, the Project's mainframe computer, crackled with malevolence as he approached. It spoke

'Thames. I have a new mission for you and Zoey.' Thames looked up sharply,

'Zoey? I thought she was through with the Leaps. After the last failed attempt, and the fact she got shot I had assumed...'

'You are not employed to assume Thames. Zoey has been given a final chance. One last mission to prove her usefulness to this Project.'

'I see. What is the mission?'

'As you are fully aware, I conceived this Project to specifically to undo the damage to the Time lines that Project Quantum Leap has been responsible for. Putting wrong what once when right so to speak. Correcting the meddling of Doctor Beckett and his amateurish hacks'

'indeed'

'It has come my attention that there is a much greater danger out there. An entity that operates way beyond the geographical limitations of this planet. One who has been meddling on a much larger scale. It is this individual that I wish for yourself and Zoey to...remove from the time lines and leave us free to continue our work here uninhibited. I have run a trillion temporal scenarios and calculated that this individual can be eliminated if we alter one specific event in the near future. I have uploaded the pertinent mission briefing into your Com Link. Zoey has been briefed and implications of any consequences pertaining to failure have been...made clear to her. She is currently in the accelerator waiting to be leapt into her subject. Go now and wait for the subject to arrive in the waiting area and then proceed to the imaging room to assist'

'Yes Sir'

'Oh and Thames'

'Yes Lothos'

'Responsibility for any failure in this will be shared equally between you both'

'I understand'

That was earlier. Thames has just come out of the Waiting room. The man in there seemed normal enough. Slightly lost, but none the worse for the transfer. He had left him singing songs about cities in Austria. No matter. He was of no importance. What was important now was to get to the Imaging Room and assist Zoey in sabotaging the computer systems on Phobos. The prospect of the Project expanding it's field of operations "Off Planet" and the mission to eliminate a thousand year old alien time traveller paled against the prospect of what Lothos would do to them if they failed. Again.

.15.
Every Little Thing She does Is Magic
The Police
1981

<<SWEEP IN 00:28:15...00:28:14...00:28:13>>

    Currently residing in Colbak's body, Zoey shifted uncomfortably. Leaping was all very well and good, but sometimes residual traits carried through from the host body. In this case a trapped sciatic nerve was niggling away at her. The mission was going smoothly, the sweeps has been sabotaged and the feedback had worked like a charm. The Facility had locked down and now it was only a matter of time before the Sweep would wipe out all life on this base. Thames had said there was a 95% probability now that the main authorities back on Earth would view this terrible tragedy as the final nail in the coffin of their Time Program and shut it down. Mission success. Zoey wasn't sure how this would ultimately destroy this man calling himself the Doctor but to be honest she didn't really care. All that mattered was that she registered a successful mission and got back in Lothos's good books. She was all prepared to Leap back out when that infernal Sam Beckett appeared on the scene. As the Doctor himself no less. Damn the man! Before Thames had left to brief Lothos, he had told her that the probability of success had fallen to 76%. Beckett's influence no less. Oh how she would love to just put a knife into Beckett's back right now...

    'Now, now Zoey, I know what you are thinking but Lothos has other plans for Doctor Beckett' Thames had just reappeared behind her as she observed the others discovering the truth about the Leap.

    'Thames. What took you so long? What did Lothos say about Beckett?' she hissed

'Lothos says it is an inconvenience at most . Don't fret about it. The mission stays the same. However we need to get Sam and Amy out of the base and back onto his time ship. Pronto. Lothos doesn't want him anywhere where he can alter the plan'

'How do I get him out of the base? Everything is on lockdown remember. That was the whole point you idiot!'

'That, Sweetcakes, is what you are employed for. Just get him out of here. Oh, and Lothos said to remind you that you are on probation'

'Yes, thanks I am well aware of that'

'Well aware of what?' said Marstrik, taking her by surprise, 'Talking to yourself? Sylmac was right it seems. Maybe Davten does have something in this memory wipe after all'. Zoey turned to face the small man who had appeared behind her.

'Marstrik. You shouldn't sneak up on people like that you know. I thought you were in your quarters waiting for the Sweep?'

'Couldn't rest Colbak. I am quite happy to wait out here. I have made peace with the situation. The loss of the last three years memory will be tough but it's the risk we all took. It will be nice to return to Earth to be honest'. Little does he know , thought Zoey to herself. But this ginger idiot could ruin everything by being out here.

'Marstrik. Actually I am glad you are here. I wanted to show you something before the Sweep starts. I would value your opinion on it before we end up forgetting each other entirely. It's in my quarters.'

'Might as well Colbak, though you will have forgotten my opinion in a few minutes anyway' he laughed as he lead the way to Colbak's small living area. 'Right so what was….' But that was as far as he got, as Zoey slammed Marstrik's head into the white panelled wall and he crumpled to the floor unconscious, a red streak of blood marking his trail down the wall.

'Ooh you are so nasty!' squealed Thames from behind her. 'I love it!'

'Sleep well' Zoey laughed as she closed the door behind her. A plan had formed in her mind.

'Thames, when I deactivated all the door palm scanners, did I leave my…I mean Colbak's registered? . Thames tapped away at the small glass looking pyramid shaped Com link in his hand.

'Yes. Should still work'

'Right. Lets get on with it then' Zoey walked back into the main Recreation room where Sam and Amy were talking to thin air. Zoey now knew that it must be. Beckett's Observer.

She walked up to Sam.

'Doctor? Davten sent me to find you. I am Colbak. I think I can help you.' Sam whispered to Al,

'Colbak?' Al tapped away on his communicator

'Colbak….wait a minute. Ah yes. Ziggy says he is a Temporanaut ….er a Time traveller at the institute. Been here two years. Has a penchant for cats and eighties music. Ziggy says he gets his mind wiped along with the rest of you…us…I mean them' Sam looked up,

'Err yes. Hi. You can help?'

'Yes indeed. I think I can get you back to your vehicle. I presume its outside the main doors in the Landing Bay' Sam confirmed it was after a quick affirmation from Al. 'Good. Follow me, both of you' Amy spoke,

'I'm not leaving without Rory'

The Doctor in Sam's body spoke

'Go with him Pond. You will be safe back in the TARDIS..stop looking at me. Play along with this please. Nobody else can see me remember.'

Al added, 'Sam, go with him. If he can get you on board this Tardy thing, go with it. I will explain more when you get there. Ziggy is fairly sure you need to be there'

'Fairly sure?' Sam hissed

'Pardon?' Zoey asked innocently

'Oh, err Fairly sure we should go with him Amy'

'Right, follow me' Zoey called as she led them back out into the Induction room, red light flooding in from the opening doorway. Al pressed a button and the door to the Imaging room opened behind him.

'Sam, I'll meet you there. I ..just need to check something with Gooshie. You wait here Doctor'

'Aye-Aye Admiral. Doctor Beckett. I know this is a lot to comprehend, but trust me if you can get back to the TARDIS, I am pretty sure we can fix this'

Sam was open to any advice at the moment and grabbed Amy's hand, pulling her after the running Colbak.

'Come on Amy'

***

In a small storage locker just beyond the recreation area, the comatose body of Davten slumped uncomfortably, where Zoey had stowed him minutes earlier.

***

Amy, Sam in the Doctor's body and Zoey in Colbak's arrived at the familiar main doorway. The echoing of their footfalls fading up the corridor. The hologram image of the Doctor in Sam's body appeared behind them. He disappeared, running through the door and then his arm reappeared waggling his fingers, before his whole body came back, running back through again.

'Ha, this is quite fun. Come along, the TARDIS is the other side of this door. My she looks beautiful. I wondered if I'd see her again'. He disappeared back to the other side of the door again like a ghost.

'Is he always like this?' whispered Sam.

'Pretty much' confirmed Amy. Zoey pretended that she didn't hear them.

'Right. I Need you both to find a hidden pressure switch in one of the walls' Zoey lied, 'Feel with your fingers . While Sam and Amy were distracted on either wall, hands spread on the walls, Zoey surreptitiously pressed her palm against the reader. The door protested slightly as it fought against the Lockdown signals it was receiving form the mainframe, before is began to rise. 'Well done, you found the switch crowed Zoey, as Amy and Sam rushed through. Sam turned back and saw Colbak remaining on the other side of the threshold.

'Colbak, Are you coming?'

'No Doctor. I must remain here. I am the Facility medic and my place is with my team', Zoey smiled inwardly at the smoothness of her lies.

'Very slick babycakes. Lothos says the probability of the doctor being erased just rose to 99.1 percent. Get ready to Leap out' Thames chimed, unheard and unseen by Sam. Sam moved towards Colbak and reached for his hand to shake it.

'I understand. I wouldn't leave my team either. Thank you'

'Don't let him touch you!' shrieked Thames, but it was too late. Sam had grabbed Colbak's hand and at that moment the temporal energies of both Leapers cancelled each other out. For a split second, each of them saw their real faces. Sam's eyes widened in horror,

'Zoey!' But before he could react, Zoey shoved Sam in the chest, hard and caught off guard, he flew back onto his backside against the blue wooden door of the Police box he had emerged from earlier.

'Too late Doctor Beckett' Zoey shouted as the door began to shut. 'I will have to kill you another time darling. I have done what I came here to do'. The body of Colbak blew him a kiss as Sam watched red neon, crackling light cover his face and arms as Zoey, the Evil Leaper, left his body. The large metal door slammed shut again.

The Doctor poked his head through the TARDIS door and looked down at Sam propped up against it.

'Come on Doctor Beckett. No time for a rest'. Al chose that moment to reappear.

'Sam. Gooshie was right. We are detecting the signature of another Leaper. We couldn't pinpoint it before because of the Doctor's proximity. That's why I had to leave him here to be sure. Sam I think the Evil Leapers could be involved here'. He looked at Sam who was staring at him, 'What?'

.16.
Don't Stop Believin'
Journey
1981

<<SWEEP IN 00:23:05...00:23:04...00:23:03>>

Al folded his arms and took a draw from his stubby cigar. Shaking his head he gave a sideways surreptitious look at Amy's legs.

'Stop it Admiral', admonished Amy, though only with a feigned amused anger. Al gave a hurt "What?" look, then he chuckled as he watched the two doctors arguing across from them. The Doctor was waving his arms at Sam,

'Do you know the mess that uncontrolled Time Travel can cause? Can you even comprehend the concept of fixed points in time?' The Time Lord ranted.

'All I know is this. I can't sit by and let all these people lose their minds. '

It had been five minutes since Colbak had pushed Sam through the door. Sam quickly explained to Al about Zoe and to the Doctor all about the Evil Leaper program. How they had run into them a few leaps previously. How they were run by a parallel organisation to Project Quantum Leap and seemed intent on undoing all the things that Sam had previously put right. He explained how in their previous meeting, Sam had shot Zoe to save another Leaper, Alia, from being killed by her.

Al had returned with information of his own. Much to the Doctor's cynicism, he explained how Ziggy had figured out what Sam was here to do. Originally in the time line, the Doctor had shut down the facility himself. He had let the Sweep take its course and allowed the short term memory of the Facility team get wiped . The Doctor had maintained that if he had indeed done this, then he would have had a good reason. Probably to stop humans meddling in time for their own good but he certainly wouldn't have let them have their minds permanently erased. That wouldn't have been him. Sam had countered that the presence of the Evil leapers meant that they had corrupted the event to ensure the Facility got shut down for some reason. Al finished by saying that Ziggy had calculated that Sam was here to stop the Sweep and allow the Newman Phillips Institute to continue its work in Time travel. The Doctor maintained that the "Safe" Sweep should be allowed to continue and that the Institute should be shut down and he was right to do so. That's when the current argument began....

'Dr Beckett, this isn't the first time I have had to do something like this. Once, on Earth there was a spatial time rift that appeared in a small side street in London. It allowed a man, to travel between the 1990's and the 1940's. Innocent enough you may think but he made changes, largely motivated by his own libido as it turns out, but changes none the less. Small changes but small changes can cause big problems. I discovered the rift by accident whilst visiting dear old Winnie in the war office and I sealed it off. But it trapped this man in 1945. By then he had become a fixed point and I couldn't rescue him. Something about one of his descendants, I can't remember exactly. I can only assume he had a good life back there. Sparrow his name was. Good bloke. Smashing bloke, but certainly no angel...no angel', the Doctor looked thoughtful for a second, 'hmm Sparrow... angels...I wonder? No. Couldn't be. Anyway my point is this, if you are not disciplined, time travel can be abused. And the Human race is not disciplined Dr Beckett. No way near ....present company excluded'

'How do you know these people will abuse it?' Sam countered 'You can't make that decision for them'

'Because people always do. I once had to confiscate a map of temporal wormholes from a gang of thieves. They weren't evil as such. Lovely guys really, really knew how to party. But they were looting history. Nice chaps but hardly people you could look up to. Well, you couldn't actually. Not one of them was above three foot nine. It's all about cause and effect. Steal a painting in Napoleonic France, and a suddenly now a servant gets fired, loses his life, never has a son, who never grows up to discover a vaccine….it escalates'. The Doctor threw up his hands and walked through the TARDIS console without appearing to notice. Sam followed him round to the other side of the console.

'I know all about that. I have made those small changes myself. I have helped change history for the better. Maybe not for the world but certainly for the world of those individuals I Leap into, and those people around them. I can't explain it but my changes correct past mistakes. Who's to say that history has to be the way it is? I make a positive difference goddammit!'

'I'm not saying it's ideal. They will survive though, they will be re-educated, given new lives. More importantly they will forget all about Time travel'. The Doctor and Sam were now standing almost nose to nose.

'How can you look at yourself in the mirror?' challenged Sam.

'At least I CAN look at myself in the mirror', retorted the Doctor with an angry smile. Amy had had enough.

'Boys! Boys! Stop it, this isn't getting anywhere', she exclaimed. Al chipped in,

'Sam, Ziggy says there is an 87% probability that you are here to stop the facility getting their brains permanently Swiss cheesed. In his time line...,' Al gestured towards the Doctor,'... the Sweep thing was completed and fifty seven people lost their entire identity. One of them, a young woman named...Bonlang ends up have a psychotic episode back on earth in 2162 and ends up blowing up a nuclear facility in Yemen. Autopsy reports suggest that severe brain damage caused by an unknown particle eraser in her past had made her go *Loco*' Sam pointed to Al, while still locked in a stare with the Doctor.

'You see. This is why I am here. To stop you from shutting this facility down. You allowed the Sweep to continue and it caused a nuclear explosion on Earth.

'There are always consequences Dr Beckett. This is what I am trying to say. How many more catastrophes would be caused by allowing this facility to continue blundering about in the time stream?'

'There's more Sam', Al continued, ' Ziggy also says, and I'm not entirely sure what this means, but he says that if allowed to continue to operate, the Newman Phillips Institute goes on to become universally known as something called the Time Agency?' The Doctor looked sharply at Al

'Say that again?'

'The Time Agency...furthermore Ziggy says, that by ultimately failing to allow the creation of this Time Agency, you jeopardise your own personal time line Doctor and you...'

'... will cease to exist' finished the Doctor quietly. Amy looked at him.

'What does that mean? What's the Time Agency?'

'It's something I am inextricably linked too. If the Time Agency, no matter how I feel about them as an entity, never gets created, then my personal time line will fall in on itself. Paradox upon paradox. Damn, how did I not spot this?' He looked at the TARDIS console.

'Admiral, that last bit wasn't Ziggy. There is no way he would be able to predict that. It's the TARDIS communicating through Ziggy to you. Aren't you old girl? You are trying to tell me. Warn me. Getting me to undo a mistake I haven't even made yet. You've seen it haven't you? You are breaking all the rules of Time you do know that?...well of course you do.' He went to pat the console affectionately but his hologram hand passed through it. He turned to Sam, who spoke,

'You see Doctor. Maybe it's not just these people in the Facility I am here to help. Maybe I am here to save you too.'

'Alright... maybe. But this doesn't change anything Dr Beckett. Even if we wanted to stop the Sweep now, we can't physically get to the fifty seven people on this station in time now. They will all have their memory wiped. I have ....been an old fool.' Amy spoke,

'Don't you dare! Don't you dare give up. You don't do that. You will think of something!....please' she pleaded. The Doctor walked over to her and looked her in the eye.

'Amy. I am so sorry. This mad man with a box has run out of time. I've finally made that one error too many. One I can't correct.

You will be safe in here. The Sweep wont be able to penetrate the TARDIS walls, but I can't say for certain what will happen next. If my own time line is about to crumble, that means we wont be here. You wont be here. We won't have ever met'

'I don't understand. How will this Time Agency thing affect you?'

'I have had many encounters with them in my past Amy. Not all of them good...sometimes they have even helped...a bit. But basically they are inextricably linked to my time line. Them and their infernal Vortex manipulators. If we...if I cause them to no longer exist, then I put my own time line in a paradox. If I am lucky, all that will happen is that I wind up with ridiculous teeth and an impractically long scarf...again. Worst case scenario is that the time line just wont be able to snap back and I cease to exist all together. Excised from time'

'Then I won't forget you Raggedy Man. I brought you back before, I can do it again' Amy said defiantly.

'No. You wont Pond, because you will never have met me. Who knows what will happen to the Time line's once I am excised from them. Time is in flux. Flapping about like a loose tarpaulin in a hurricane. Even your enormous leap of faith wouldn't bring me back this time.'

All this time Sam was stood leaning forward on the console. Head down with both hands clutching at the raised counter. Not in a dissimilar position to the one he was in when he first arrived here. At the Doctor's last words his head shot up,

'Did you say leap of faith?' he said excitedly

'Hmm?' said the Doctor sadly, still staring solemnly at his flame haired companion.

'The Sweep lasts for one minute right? Sam asked.

'Yes. We heard Tic-Toc. No escape. The wave hits you, and in that sixty seconds it erases your mind. Brilliantly effective, if completely barbaric'

'What if their minds weren't there to be erased? The others looked at him blankly. Al spoke up,

'Err Sam. I think you've had a long day. Take a seat over there and...'

'No Listen. Shut up a minute Al. Hear me out'

'Charming'

'Just listen to me. If their minds are not in their bodies, then the Sweep won't have anything to erase. It will pass through them harmlessly'

'Yeah, Brilliant Sam. Small problem though. They DO actually have their minds' Al was worried that this Leap was sending Sam over the sanity ledge. Even if you seem to have lost yours' he added.

'Right, but what if they Leaped out at the moment that the Sweep starts and they Leaped back in after it finished?' Sam looked at the Doctor and back at Al.' I have seen enough technology here that I think I can replicate a Leap Accelerator. Facility wide. I could leap them all out. Leave the body here but leap the mind to safety, beyond the reach of the Sweep'

'Sam, are you nuts? Even if you could leap them all out, they would be lost in time like you. You would be achieving zip! They'd be as good as lobotomised anyway. You can't control your own Leaps, what makes you think you could Leap them back again? Who are you even going to Leap them into for this magic minute? Whoever you Leap them into would be back here in their place. You'd be sacrificing fifty seven new victims.' Sam looked crestfallen but the Doctor joined in.

'Themselves. You could Leap them into themselves but one minute into their own future. You wouldn't need to Leap them back. They would lose one minute of their life sure, but that's better than losing it all. Doctor Becket that is genius. Normally I don't use that to describe someone else in the same room as me but that really is genius.' Sam interrupted him,

'But Al's right Doctor. I could Leap them out but Ziggy couldn't handle the calculations involved to Leap fifty seven people simultaneously into themselves. I don't even know how to do it myself. That's how I got into this mess in the first place.'

'No, Ziggy definitely couldn't, but the TARDIS could! In fact the TARDIS could replicate the entire process if you operated it. With my help of course!'

'Doctor. I can't even begin to understand how to operate the TARDIS' The Doctor walked over to Sam and lifted his fedora.

'Doctor Beckett. Leave that to me. Admiral, may I borrow that hand link please? I will be a few moments.' Al, looked from one doctor to the other. Then at Amy. Then gave up and tossed his communicator across the imaging chamber to the Doctor. The Doctor pressed a button and a luminous doorway slid open behind him. 'Don't go anywhere' he said with a wink, pointing to them all in turn with a grin on his face a mile wide. He then disappeared through the portal with a final 'Ha-haa!' and vanished. Al waited for him to go before speaking,

'Sam, there's something else....there is more than one time bomb counting down here...'

.17.
The Return of the Los Palmas (Fifty) Seven
Madness
1981

<<SWEEP IN 00:03:45...00:03:44...00:03:43>>

The Doctor reappeared in the TARDIS console room, this time in addition to his already eclectic ensemble he was now wearing a pair of red lensed wrap around spectacles.

'Will you please stay out of my god damn wardrobe locker!' exclaimed Al. The Doctor ignored him and turned to Sam.

'Are you ready Dr Beckett?' Sam looked at him with a concerned frown

'No, not really Doctor. I told you, I have no idea how to operate your TARDIS. These controls are frankly...well ridiculous'

'I shall pretend I didn't hear that' the Doctor snorted and then into the hand link he said, 'If you are ready Mr Gooshie? Now if you please' The voice of the diminutive programmer could be heard squeaking that he was ready and a holographic beam of light lit up one half of the TARDIS console. Although the control panel could be seen below it, overlaying the controls were holographic representations of controls and displays screens that Sam instantly recognised.

'Hey! I know this. This is the control system from the Quantum Leap Facility Relay Room. How did you do this?' Sam enthusiastically walked round the TARDIS console, giving out small laughs and exclamations of recognition as he surveyed his familiar workstation. The Doctor joined him.

'Easy, I asked Mr Gooshie to digitise the control panels you are used to working with and, with my help, we have overlaid them onto the equivalent control panels on my TARDIS in the form of a holographic projection. It isn't an exact match as you don't have an equivalent of a Bi-Dimensional Compression Transponder in your time, but it should be close enough to achieve the desired results. I will operate the necessary time and space calculations and adjustments from this side of the console'

'Brilliant!'

'I know, right?', the Doctor went to straighten his bowtie and looked slightly crestfallen when he realised he wasn't wearing it. Sam compounded his disappointment by straightening his.

'But how are you going to touch your controls. You are still a hologram' chipped in Al

'Oh well aren't you the raincloud of doom Admiral' harrumphed the Doctor, chucking the hand link communicator back to Al, who caught it at the expense of dropping his cigar. 'Don't panic, I have these little beauties!'

The Doctor pulled out a pair of thin white gloves from his jacket pocket. They had veins of neon blue light running down the length of each finger. He pulled them over each hand and waggled his fingers at Amy whilst waggling his eyebrows. 'These are Tactile Hologram Interactive Neural Gain Yielders ...or T.H.I.N.G.Y.s ... Actually that sounds rubbish now I say that out loud. Anyway, the name isn't important. I have knocked these up to enable me to touch the TARDIS controls from here inside the imaging chamber. Now stop distracting me. Us Doctors have work to do. Doctor Beckett, shall we?'

'Where did you get those?' asked Al

'I made them. I found some bits and bobs lying around the place. Anyway, now is not the time. Doctor Beckett?'

<<SWEEP IN 00:02:17...00:02:16...00:02:15>>

Sam had already started however. Hesitantly at first, but growing in confidence the more he got used to operating the dual controls in front of him.

'This is incredible', he muttered as he span a wheel on the TARDIS console that corresponded to the sliding switch that he had designed back on Earth on his control bank. 'Doctor, I think we can actually do this, but I need to be able to locate the people in the Facility.

'I'm on it. Just let me...there. Right they should be appearing on your screen now. Got them?'

'Yes. I have them. All 57'

'57. Heinz Varieties. 57 Human Beans haha!'

Amy came up behind him. 'You mean 58. Don't forget Rory' the Doctor slapped his forehead.

'Yes of course. I used the Facility's Personnel database to find them all, but Rory wouldn't be on there would he? Wait a moment, just need to scan for life signs, Facility wide...there he is. What's he doing way down there? Never mind. Do you have him Doctor Beckett?

'Yes I've got him. 58 Leapers ready to Leap. Are you sure that we can Leap them back into themselves?. I have replicated my experiment, but...obviously it didn't quite work as I envisaged the first time round.' He looked up at the Doctor. The Doctor hesitated before speaking,

'Yes, the TARDIS can do it. She has compensated for the miscalculations in your original computations all those years ago and it's now a complete working theory. Doctor Beckett. But I can't let you see it I'm afraid. I know what you are thinking. Please. Don't ask me'

'But if I could just see the calculations, I might be able to figure out a way to get back home' Sam implored. The Doctor sighed, but before he could answer Amy shouted,

'Can you two hear actually the countdown?' she pleaded,' If you are going to do something you have to do it now!' Al clicked his hand held communicator and added,

'Sam, she's right, if you want to Leap you have to do this now!' Sam held the Doctor's gaze for a second longer before, looking down at the panel,

<<SWEEP IN 00:00:13...00:00:12...00:00:11>

'Fine. Of course you are right' Ok, I'm ready. In 3...2...' The Doctor joined in on the countdown,

'...1....Geronimooo...'

...OOhhhh Boy!'

Both men slammed a control on their respective keypads and the TARDIS began to shake

<<SWEEP COMMENCING...SWEEP COMMENCING...SWEEP COMMENCING>>>

Suddenly the Doctor fell to the ground clutching at his head in obvious pain.

'Arrrrghh! It's no use I can't...'. The Doctor collapsed to the floor unconscious. Amy rushed over to him but her hands passed right through the hologram. Al knelt down by him and felt for a pulse.

'He's still alive Sam, but it's as I feared. The Doctor isn't human, I mean he's got a double pulse for godsake, but it's his mind. Sam whatever he is, he has an incredibly complicated mind and, don't take offence here, but I don't think your brain can quite contain it. I've been watching this guy since he got here and he has been complaining of headaches. I got Gooshie to run some scans and I think the Doctor's mind is destroying your brain. You need to Leap out and let them back in his body a-sap'

'What's happened with the Sweep. Has it worked?' Sam countered. 'If that's what I am here to do then, if its worked I should be Leaping?

'Hold on, err Ziggy says yes, your plan worked. All 58 people were leaped out and ...in 5...4...3...2....1.. they have all leaped back. You did it Sam! The Sweep is finished and they all still have their memories and 100% of their brain function intact...with a 5% margin of error. Ziggy says history has changed and the Newman Phillips Institute continues into the 51st Century!'

'That's great Al, but why am I still here?'

'Ziggy says...err , come on you stupid...ah Ziggy says that the percentages are in flux and that's not all you were here to do. You need to find Rory Williams'

'Damn right we do!' shouted Amy, who had remained silent since the Doctor collapsed.

'Come on Sam, Ziggy can lead us to him. You too Legs. You need to be there too'

'Try and stop me'

.18.
Keep On Loving You
REO Speedwagon
1981

'Turn right here Sam', Al appeared at the intersection in front of them as they approached it, running up from an umpteenth, unremarkable corridor. Amy had shown Sam the correct setting for the Sonic Screwdriver and the Facility doors were opening up before them as if they were melting into the walls at their approach.

'How is he doing that?' asked Amy, slightly out of breath.

'Doing what?' Sam replied, also feeling the strain of their progress on his lungs.

'Appearing ahead of us like that all the time. We leave him at one door and then he appears up ahead.'

'Ah, well, Ziggy is centering Al in the Imaging Chamber back on Earth at stage points along our route. It means Al can keep up with us, and show us the way to the Launch Bays without having to actually run with us'

'Lucky Al' she muttered, puffing.

'It's a little hard to comprehend. Al is actually in a tiny room, but to him its like he has the whole world in there with him. Sounds weird huh?'

'Err, You have seen the TARDIS right?'

'Oh. Yeah. I suppose you are right' Sam conceded, recalling his amazement at the size of the blue box's interior.

They eventually came to a large open rotunda where half a dozen people were milling about in dazed confusion. Nobody challenged their presence, and a few just stared at them blankly before looking at their hands, rubbing their foreheads of talking to each other in hushed, befuddled voices. Al appeared from across the large expanse and waved at them,

'Over here Sam. This is Bay Seven'. They made the last dash swiftly and with a quick flash of the screwdriver, the door unsealed to let them in. Amy ran in first with Sam close behind. Sat against the opposite wall, a shell shocked Rory Williams looked up as his wife appeared in the room like a vision. He stood up, shaking his head,

'Amy? I knew you would come. Are you ok? Do you still remember me?' Amy said nothing as she walked over to him and wrapped her arms around him in an embrace that a boa constrictor would have been proud of.

'Of course I remember you. Shut up you idiot.'

'Ah yes. Clearly you do remember me' he gasped as the air was squeezed from his chest.

'Rory? What is all that on the wall?'

Behind Rory on the wall was a jumble of hand written words, and half sentences. Place names, people, and dates. There was even a five bar gate.

River Song Lake Silencio **Mels** *Hitler* Venice

Prisoner Zero Pandorica *Last Centurion*, Waiting,

102 C.E White House **Kovarian** Wedding *Dinosaurs*
Leadworth Melody Pond, **Royal Leadworth Hospital** Eknodine,

Cwmtaff, Stonehenge, **Honeymoon Suite** Starship, **Siren**, Apalapucia ||||

'I err, thought I might lose all my memories of you in that sweep thing. So I spent a few minutes writing down every memory I had of you. Of everything we have done in case it might help me remember. Then I stopped.'

'Why?'

'Because I realised that none of those things mattered. I love you, and I have done since I first laid eyes on you. I realised that even if I forgot you completely, and I even if I forgot me completely, as soon as I laid eyes on you again I knew would fall in love with you all over again. Build new memories...' She cut him off with a hard kiss on the lips.

'Aww ain't young love wonderful Sam?' cooed Al watching the scene with Sam at the doorway, ' Reminds me of me and Beth when we first met. Didn't quite have those legs though...'

'Al, why haven't I Leaped? The Doctor is dying back there remember? In my body. What does Ziggy say now?' Al snapped out of his reverie and took out his communicator,

'Oh, yeah right. Well, Ziggy hasn't a clue. The percentages are all over the place. All I can get from him is it's something to do with the wall scribbler over there'

'Rory? What about Rory?' Sam walked over to the couple.

'Rory, what's happened here?' Rory looked up from his wife's gaze,

'Oh hello Doctor. Well...' Amy interrupted.

'That's not the Doctor. It's a long story, but he's in the Doctor's body and the Doctor is in his body back on Earth. And he is dying. It's complicated but we need to find out what Sam...him, is here to correct so that they can swap back. ' Rory blinked

'Correct? I don't understand' , Sam grabbed him by the shoulders.

'Something went wrong here the first time around. I am here to put it right.'

'Sam, Ziggy says you all need to be back in the TARDIS. Now!'

'Ok. Whatever he says. We need to get back to the TARDIS. Now. Hurry.' Sam let Rory and Amy go first out the door and he had a quick glance around at the Launch bay before he went with them. There wasn't much to see. A small Pod was against one wall, and it looked like there had once been another next to it. Its outline was scorched into the wall. Sam sighed. He had no idea what he was looking for. Just as he turned to go, something caught his eye. Al urged his friend,

'Come on Sam. We need to hoof it outta here. What is it?' Sam had bent down to pick up a folded piece of paper that was on the floor by where Rory had been sitting. He unfolded it and read the writing on it. Sam noted two separate sets of hand writing. One had some instructions and a personal note to Rory, The other set was on the back of the paper and was a few lines written in the same style as the writing on the wall. It read,

'Your name is Rory Williams. If you escape this, you must tell the Doctor about Hila Tacorien. Find out if she made it. Make sure she is safe'

'Sam, That's it! I don't know what that is you've got there, but Ziggy has just gone ballistic. Says there's now a 98.9 percent probability that you are meant to tell the Doctor about this Hila Tacorien broad. Ziggy says, in the original history, Rory, in his relief at being rescued and reunited with Legs, forgets to tell the Doctor about her. Also that may be due to him having had his head partially Swiss cheesed in that stunt you and the Doc just pulled. He intended to give that paper to the Doctor but he never did. Sam, don't lose that paper!'

Sam, folded it up carefully and put it in the inside pocket of his jacket, next to the wallet object he found so many hours before.

'Don't worry Al, I'll make sure he....'

But that was as far as he got. The all to familiar, neon blue light poured over him as Sam Beckett Leaped out of the Doctor's body.

'Well I'll be...' muttered Al as the Doctor straightened up slowly, back in his own body

'Oooh that feels so much better. Headache gone. Both hearts are pumping. Bow tie back under chin! Oh, hello Admiral. You worked it out then? Good man. Knew you would. No don't tell me what it was. I don't need to know. Just tell me where the Ponds went if you would.'

'Welcome back Doc', Al smiled.' Love's young dream went that way' he pointed with his cigar. 'Sorry I can't stay. Got to find Sam again. Listen, before I go. Was it true what you told me earlier? The bit about Sam never going home?' The Doctor sighed sadly

'I fear so Admiral. But don't tell him hey? I think it best for him to keep hope don't you?' Al nodded as he closed his eyes.

'Gooshie has speculated as much for some time now. But yes, don't worry. Sam doesn't need to know that. I doubt he would accept it anyway'

'Probably not' agreed the Doctor,

'Whatever happens though, I will be with him to keep him moving along. He's a good kid.'

'You both are Admiral. Despite what I said to Doctor Beckett earlier in the TARDIS, he is doing good. Meddling can be done for the right reasons and still turn out for the best. I'd be lying if I said I followed my own rules all of the time. Anyway, don't tell anyone I said this, but I have been wrong before you know.' he winked at Al. ' Never say never about returning home. What do I know? I am just a mad man with a box. Right onwards and upwards. I think I need to pay a visit to a certain other Evil Facility at some point. Putting wrong what once went right is not something I am comfortable with allowing to continue hmm?'

'Thanks Doc. That would sure help. Those Evil Leapers are a menace. Anything you can do would be great'

'It's a promise Admiral. The least I can do'

'Take care Doc. Say goodbye to Legs for me' Al punched a key on his communicator and the door to the imaging chamber slid open.

Al stepped through it. 'Ziggy ? Where's Sam this time...' he said as the door closed and he was gone.

The Doctor gave a small sigh,

'Farewell Admiral. Go easy on the Cubans', before running out of the door to the Launch Bay

'Ponds! I'm Back!'

Epilogue
Fade to Grey
Visage
1981

Amy walked round the console to where the Doctor was adjusting the TARDIS display monitor.

'I know you could have helped Sam if you had wanted to', she said. 'Why didn't you?'

The Doctor looked down and fiddled with a small dial absent mindedly. He sighed.

'Dr Beckett is supposed to be doing what he is doing. I know, I know. It's not fair, but he's a fixed point in time...well not fixed because he keeps moving about. He's a moving fixed point. I can't change that.' The Doctor paused, then he looked up at Amy.

'There was a time when my people, the Time Lords, made it their job to police Time. To stop the blunderings of so called, lesser species when they dared to experiment in time travel. They had the right intentions, or so I used to think. Time travel is dangerous. It is too easy to cause catastrophe just by simply being in the wrong time or saying the wrong thing. Breathing the wrong breath. Ripples... Ha!' he said to the air. 'Someone very clever once said something very wise about the ripples we create with every decision...it might have been me actually', he sighed wistfully.

'With no more Time Lords left, it's just me. But I can't police the whole universe Amy. I'm not sure I would want to anyway. Human endeavour...well any species endeavour really, is what makes life wonderful. We Time Lords wouldn't even be Time Lords had we not experimented. Poked a Black Hole with a stick and saw what happened. Nobody tried to stop us back then. Doctor Beckett isn't alone you know. I do know of others. For every Beckett or indeed Newman or Phillips, there is an, a Pilgrim or a Nakamura. There are Sparrows, Slades, Tylers and Mallorys. The universe is a big place

Pond. Room enough for all maybe. By and large they are all good people. Who am I to stop them? In Doctor Beckett's case I can't help him anyway. He has to do what he does. Fated if you like... not that I believe in fate. In all honesty he could actually go home anytime he likes, he just has to work that bit out for himself. It's not something that I could , or should ever show him'. He saw the mild disapproving look on Amy's face. He walked over to her and put an arm around her shoulder.

'If it helps, think of it like this. Sam Beckett is wandering through time, helping the people he meets and improving their lives in small but significant ways. Sometimes in large, significant ways. It is wholly unfair because he never stays for any thanks or gratitude, and he can never go home' Amy looked back at him with a strange expression. 'What?' The Doctor asked

'Sounds like someone else I know' she said quietly with a smile

She leant over and kissed his forehead before walking away up the stairs where Rory was waiting for her. He was muttering something about losing a piece of paper but not remembering why it was important.

The Doctor smiled, leant across the console and pressed a small red button. A small bell rang twice. He cranked a small handle and outside in the swirling vortex, the rectangular black sign atop the blue box rotated from Police Public Call Box to NOT IN SERVICE

'Tickets please! Please Don't Distract your driver! Next stop…..Everywhere!'

***

Sam Beckett Leaped. He found he was sitting down this time. The memory of the last Leap was still fairly fresh in his mind but as always was already fading fast. What next? He smiled up at a woman who had just handed him what looked like a shiny acrylic clip board. She seemed to be waiting for some kind of reply.

'Err…thank you?' he said. Good manners usually papered a few cracks. That didn't seem to work though. She spoke

'What are your orders?' she said in a level, almost emotionally devoid voice. Strange ears Sam thought. Uncharacteristically quickly, Al was suddenly there right next to him.

'Er… Sam. If you thought the last Leap was loco. This one is going to be a doozy'. The mysterious woman spoke at Sam again.

'Captain Archer, your orders? Do we attack or surrender?'

Sam, looked down at the reflective surface of the clipboard and for the first time in what seemed like forever saw his own face looking back at him. He looked up at Al, who just nodded silently and gestured with his cigar for Sam to look at the scene in front of him

Space.

A Space Ship.

A Space Ship and explosions!

Sam closed his eyes again

 'Oh boy!'

***

Sometime in the future. Well one future anyway, a small blue box materialised somewhere deep under the streets of London. Inside a large white tiled room with vivid red marbling, it stood out alarmingly.

Above the blue box, an angry red globe of flickering circuits hummed loudly as the doors to the blue box opened with a soft creak. A man walked out. The red inner lining of his black coat complemented the baleful red glow of the tiles. His wild silver hair was matched only by the severity of his eyebrows. He looked up at the ceiling globe and then down at another man who came scurrying up to him.

'Who are you?' said, recently demoted, Project Technician Gamma Level Thames

'Sorry I'm late. I've been meaning to come here for some time. Got a bit waylaid on Trenzalore, you know how it is. Shut up. Wait. You must be Thames right? I've heard all about you That's unlucky. For you. And your friend up there is Lothos, am I right again? Of course I am. Bear with me , I've only just regenerated. I've left my friend back in the Eighteen hundreds with a lizard and a potato, so I can't stop long. At least I hope she is still my friend. Shut up! Listen. I've made many mistakes, and it's about time I did something about them. Starting with you lot. You see, here's the thing. I'm not sure yet whether I am a good man or not. But. I made a promise to *a very* good man a long time ago and I think this new body has just the right amount of anger in it right now to do you boys justice. He pulled out his sonic screwdriver and advanced on a cowering Thames. 'Let's get started shall we?'

And so we, the observers, pan away and up through the layers for marble, structural steel and concrete, up through the pavements of London and further up into the cold vacuum of Space. We leave two good men to their ongoing adventures. Both setting out to put things right and both looking for a way back home....

THE END?

Alternative Ending Souvenir *Orchestral Manoeuvres in the Dark*
1981

SARAH: Get it off! Get it off!

(Sarah and Harry pull at the gelatinous thing and finally get it off the Doctor's throat. Harry throws part of it back into the incubation room, the Doctor does the same with the remainder and closes the door. They move a little way down the corridor, and the Doctor holds the two wires. Then he hesitates putting them together to close the circuit and detonate the explosives.)

SARAH: What are you waiting for?

DOCTOR: Just touch these two strands together and the Daleks are finished. Have I that right?

SARAH: To destroy the Daleks? You can't doubt it.

DOCTOR: Well, I do. You see, some things could be better with the Daleks. Many future worlds will become allies just because of their fear of the Daleks.

SARAH: But it isn't like that.

DOCTOR: But the final responsibility is mine, and mine alone. Listen, if someone who knew the future pointed out a child to you and told you that that child would grow up totally evil, to be a ruthless dictator who would destroy millions of lives, could you then kill that child?

SARAH: We're talking about the Daleks, the most evil creatures ever invented. You must destroy them. You must complete your mission for the Time Lords.

DOCTOR: Do I have the right? Simply touch one wire against the other and that's it. The Daleks cease to exist. Hundreds of millions of people, thousands of generations can live without fear, in peace, and never even know the word Dalek.

SARAH: Then why wait? If it was a disease or some sort of bacteria you were destroying, you wouldn't hesitate.

DOCTOR: But I kill, wipe out a whole intelligent lifeform, then I become like them. I'd be no better than the Daleks.

SARAH: Think of all the suffering there'll be if you don't do it.

(Blue Light Plays on the Doctor's face and hands. Electric neon energy crackles and arcs underneath the unfeasibly long knitted scarf as Sam Beckett leaps into his new body. Looking down at the two wires in his hand and the expectant look on the attractive girl's face next to him, he can only assume he is expected to make some kind of decision here. And quickly)

Doctor: Oh Boy!

Character Biographies

Al - Admiral Albert Calavicci

Al and Sam worked together in the Project Quantum Leap. When Sam stepped into the Project Accelerator too early, vanishing into the past, Al got the task of giving information to Sam and keep him in touch to his own time. He appeared to Sam as a hologram, which only Sam could see and hear, although animals, small children, "mentally absent" and people near death could see Al and Sam as he really is. Al carries the Handlink which is used to open and close the Imaging Chamber Door and keep in touch with Ziggy, the project's hybrid computer. Imaging Chamber is the room where Al goes, when he gives information to Sam.

Sam - Doctor Samuel Beckett

Samuel "Sam" Beckett invented a theory about time traveling and led a group of scientists to the desert to develop a top secret project: Quantum Leap. In pressure to prove his theories or lose funding, he stepped into the unfinished project accelerator and vanished. He soon found himself leaping into other persons' bodies in the past, correcting things that once happened wrong to them.

Sam has a photographic memory, an IQ of 267, can cook, likes dry or light beer, and microwave popcorn. Sam also knows several kinds of martial arts such as Judo, Karate, Muay Thai, and Taekwondo, and has been afraid of heights since he was 9 years old. Sam also plays the piano and guitar, is a good dancer, sings baritone, and his favourite song is John Lennon's "Imagine".

Sam speaks 7 modern languages including English, Spanish, French, Russian, German, and Japanese, but not Italian or Hebrew. He knows four dead languages, including Egyptian hieroglyphics. He has won a Nobel Prize in an unspecified field, but probably for physics. For this, Time magazine called him "the next Einstein".

Sam developed the Project Quantum Leap based on his String Theory with Al. He led a group of scientists into the New Mexico desert to develop a top secret project known as the Quantum Leap. After creating Ziggy and the Imaging Chamber, under pressure to prove his theories or lose funding, Dr. Sam Beckett stepped into the Project Accelerator and vanished.

Sam leaping for the first time in the Project Accelerator

He awoke in the past, suffering from partial amnesia and facing a mirror image that was not his own. Luckily, Al, the project observer from his own time, appeared, in the form of a Hologram to Sam. Only Sam could see or hear Al, although later it appeared that also animals, small children, the "mentally absent", and people near death could see Al and Sam the way he is. There is an aura around Sam, which makes others, except for the ones listed earlier, see Sam as the one he has leaped into. Whomever he leaps into goes to the Waiting Room, in Sam's own time, where he or she is kept by the project staff until he or she gets back when Sam leaps into the next person. These people are called Leapees.

Gooshie

Gooshie is a computer programmer and the programmer of Ziggy. He met Sam Beckett in the Starbright Project and later helped him in Project Quantum Leap.

Ziggy

Ziggy is the super hybrid computer that runs the Project Quantum Leap. It was built by Samuel Beckett and Gooshie, being one of the first creations in the Project Quantum Leap. Ziggy has a sense of humour, which many computers don't have. Sam himself said: "The only thing separating Ziggy from a normal calculating machine is his ego." In fact, he later expanded on this in the episode The Leap Back. In this episode, after Ziggy was being particularly stubborn, Sam lamented about it by saying "Why did I have to give him

Barbara Streisand's ego?" Ziggy has lots of information of the past and gives information to Al to be given to Sam. Ziggy can't express guilt, being a computer. Al uses the Handlink to keep contact with Ziggy while he is in the Imaging Chamber.

Zoey

Nothing is known from Zoey's early life. At some point she became the hologram of Alia, after she was leaped into the past, putting things wrong that once were right. When Alia escaped with Sam by leaping with him, Zoey decided to try to leap after them, and so

Lothos, the computer used by the Evil Leapers, the evil counterpart of Ziggy, leaped her into the same time where they were in. Zoey tries to kill Alia by shooting her in the end but Alia is able to leap out of the time period unharmed. When she aims her gun in a attempt to shoot Sam, he reacts quickly and shoots Zoey with another gun! Though Zoey is seen leaping, her leapee returns unharmed with the presumably fatal wound being carried by Zoey as she leaps out.

Thames

A darkly comical man, Thames became the hologram guide of Zoey, who originally the hologram guide of Alia in the episode "Deliver Us From Evil". In "Revenge of The Evil Leaper", Thames is assigned by the Evil Leapers to guide the equally evil Zoey, who was hell bent on killing Alia, who was persuaded by Sam to leave the Evil Leapers and start leaping for good. When Zoey leaps into September 1987, assuming the body of a women's prison warden, where Alia and Sam leaped into, the quirky Thames, who has a morbid sense of humour is assigned to guide her, with the use of Lothos

Lothos

Lothos is the artificial intelligence designed to run the Evil Leaper Project. Much like Ziggy, Lothos is able to predict the likely outcome of historical changes by the leapers, and observers from his present can communicate with him through a hand-held device. However, unlike Ziggy, Lothos, whose brain may be that of the presumably late Dr. Nathaniel Lothoman, who designed him, seems to be in complete control of the leaps, deciding where and when people leap to, and picking their missions. It is also implied that Lothos controls multiple Leapers at a time.

The Doctor

"The Doctor" was the primary alias of a renegade Time Lord from Gallifrey who travelled through time and space with various companions in his obsolete and "borrowed" Type 40 TARDIS. He was the universe's "greatest defender", having saved the cosmos thousands of times throughout his long life, becoming a great legend across the whole universe.

Amelia Jessica "Amy" Pond

Sometimes styled Amelia Williams after her marriage - was the first companion of the Doctor in his eleventh incarnation. She was the girlfriend and later wife of nurse Rory Williams, and the mother of Melody Pond, who later became known as River Song. Amy died aged 87 at some point prior to 2012 after allowing a Weeping Angel to send her back in time, hoping to be reunited with her husband. She was buried beside Rory in a graveyard in New York.

Rory Arthur Williams

Sometimes called Rory Pond — was Amy Pond's husband. He became a companion of the Eleventh Doctor on the night before their wedding, but he died and was erased from history after being absorbed by the Time Field. Shortly before the Pandorica was opened, Rory reappeared, in a fashion, waited for Amy to come out of the Pandorica for 1,894 years and was restored to normal after the second Big Bang. He went on to marry Amy and resumed travelling with her and the Doctor. During this time, his child, Melody Pond, was born. When the Doctor married River, Rory became his father-in-law. In 2012, he was sent back in time by a Weeping Angel, and was soon followed through time by his wife. He died at age 82 sometime before 2012. His gravestone stood in a graveyard in New York.

Printed in Great Britain
by Amazon.co.uk, Ltd.,
Marston Gate.